Mona Lisa's Secret

Color Picture Photo Edition

Bruce Davidson

Mona Lisa's Secret: Color Picture Photo Edition

ISBN – 9798344276830

Printed in the United States of America

First Edition (2024)

Amazon Publishing Company USA (Headquarters)

410 Terry Avenue N.

Seattle, Washington 98109-5210

206-266-1000

Dedication

This novel is dedicated to all those who are seekers of permanent, international peace on Earth, a place where we all must somehow learn to coexist.

The Mona Lisa at the Louvre Museum in Paris, France

Painted by Leonardo da Vinci

Table of Contents

About the Author

The author of "Bear's In Charge," Bruce Davidson, in his novel, "Mona Lisa's Secret," reveals the mystery of the enigmatic smile of the Mona Lisa at the Louvre Museum in Paris, France, created by the genius Leonardo da Vinci. Bruce is an honor graduate of a top-ranking United States university and a United States Air Force veteran working with F-4 Phantom Combat Fighter Jets. He has acted on movie sets and performed Shakespeare on stage.

Mona Lisa's Secret: Color Picture Photo Edition

1

Manhattan, New York

"It is the very error of the Moon. She comes more near the Earth than she was wont. And makes men mad."

— William Shakespeare, "Othello"

It came as no surprise to anyone in Manhattan that there was a full Moon on this ominous evening. Even the skeptical first responders, that is, the police, firefighters, EMTs, and paramedics, who may not have previously believed in the full-Moon effect prior, were beginning to think that on this particular evening, there may be something to it. Sirens were blaring all over New York City, especially in its most densely populated area, Manhattan Island. It was not a stretch to say that all hell had broken loose.

All over the world, there are many people who are convinced that the mystical powers of a full Moon, on top of triggering the tides on the beaches, induce erratic human behaviors and all manner of bizarre events. Across the centuries, many people have uttered the phrase: "There must be a full Moon out tonight," in an attempt to explain weird events having taken place at night. Indeed, the Roman goddess of the Moon bore a name that remains familiar to us all: Luna, which is where the word "lunacy" is derived. The belief that a full Moon is capable of provoking uncommon thinking is embellished by the lunar lunacy effect, hence, moonstruck.

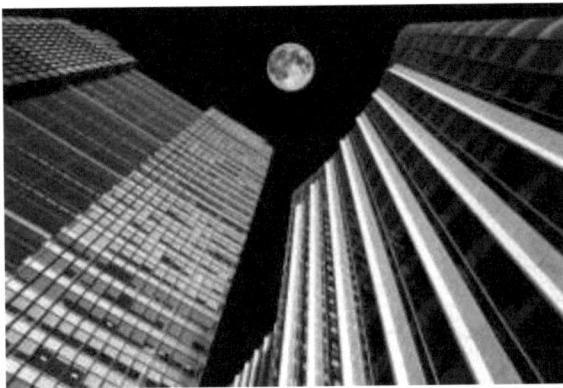

Also known as the Transylvania effect, the phenomenal lunar lunacy effect refers to the notion that human beings are widely reputed to have commonly transformed into vampires or werewolves during a full Moon. And all over Manhattan tonight, while there may not have been anyone biting into another person's neck, turning into a bat, slipping into a casket just before dawn, growing hair all over their body in the course of a few minutes, or howling at the full Moon, metaphorically and figuratively speaking, people all over the famous island of New York City, Manhattan Island, were turning into vampires and werewolves by way of their actions.

The laser beam glare and gravitational force of the Moon focused on one of the most luxurious condominium apartment buildings in Manhattan on Billionaire's Row, 432 Park Avenue, well known for its exclusive location, high-end, lavish amenities, luxurious features, and absolutely stunning, dramatic views of Central Park. The penthouse view from the top 96th floor, occupied by a billionaire, offered one the most spectacular viewpoints of New York City. Central to this focus bearing down hard from the Moon was Apartment 66-B of 432 Park Avenue, boasting an eye-level, unmatched, breathtaking, panoramic Central Park and Manhattan skyline views through a grand array of colossal, triple-paned windows. 432 Park Avenue, at 1,396 feet in height, is the third-highest residential skyscraper in the world. Located in New York City at 57th Street and Park Avenue in Midtown Manhattan, 432 Park Avenue is a two-minute taxi drive from Times Square.

It was here that Tony and Madonna Romona lived in comfortable surroundings of a 4019 square foot residence with their eighteen-year-old daughter, Mona Lisa. The apartment was rented out for $79,000 a month and had a sales value worth $29,042,362.

432 Park Avenue Condo Apartments

Sunday Evening

Normally, on a Sunday night around Romona's household, it's a relaxing, laid-back, reflective bonding time for these three close family members. But tonight, something was eerily amiss. The shimmering, oversized full Moon hung perfectly level with Romona's sixty-six-floor apartment windows for the moment, serving as a clear indicator and premonition that something quite ominous in a most palpable manner was about to have its way.

Tony Romano, an executive with a major international import/export company in New York City, and his wife, Madonna, an international affairs attorney and partner with a large, very prestigious law firm, were in a heated argument. Tony had agreed to go to church for the very first time with Madonna earlier that Sunday, attending the morning service. Madonna had been relentlessly pestering Tony to go to church for years, but Tony stubbornly refused to consent. Never in his life had Tony been a big churchgoer, and the only reason he went this Sunday morning was to get Madonna off his back once and for all and prove to her that all it would serve to accomplish was confirm his suspicions. Mona Lisa Romano, a sweet, beautiful, good-natured, brown-haired, brown-eyed senior in high school with high hopes of getting through college at NYU, had always submissively gone to church with her mother. But Mona also had many previous conversations with her father concerning his reasoning for why he refused to go. Caught between the opposing outlooks of her mother and father forced Mona to witness a serious dichotomy that instilled within her a certain degree of confusion. Tony was a highly intelligent Italian man with dark features whose main point of debate was that he didn't need to go to church after all the negative attributes he had personally observed of church people out in the community at large. Tony wasn't crazy about the idea of being trapped between the four walls of a church with these kinds of people in close proximity. He didn't need to look through a microscope to get a more vivid perception of determining his own opinion of these types of individuals. Tony felt he could clearly see through them from a safe distance.

"Madonna, how come you're missing it? You could do better than hanging out with these nuts! It would be an improvement for you to go to the country club." Tony exclaimed with great intensity.

"You're a very nice person. And these church people aren't nice at all. You have class, and they don't. In fact, they're out of touch! Can't you see that? It couldn't be more apparent! You can tell they don't even have a sense of right or wrong. Those people don't represent God!"

"Well, at least you're acknowledging God, Tony! But there are people in the church who have a lot of love." Madonna insisted.

"Have a lot of love!" Tony said with utter disdain.

"What are you talking about? Weren't you and I in the same Sunday School class together this morning? All those people were doing in there was arguing over various doctrines and banging each other over the head with the Bible. I have a serious problem with these impostors who claim to be delegates for the Lord. It doesn't take a jet rocket scientist to figure out these people are nothing but a bunch of two-faced, conniving backstabbers. You could practically see the daggers in their eyes! I felt like I was on a pirate ship this morning in that church! They're trying to dictate how you think, Madonna."

"It's called rightly dividing the word of truth, Tony," Madonna interjected.

"They are trying to sort out the truth in the Bible."

"Oh, they were rightly divided as they were sorting out the truth, all right! They could have been a little more polite with each other about it. I thought there was supposed to be unity in the church. They couldn't agree on anything!" Tony responded sarcastically, considering Madonna's reply to be lame.

"And these people tell others not to love the world. They preach that other people shouldn't be like the world. But they themselves are, literally, the worldliest and the greediest people on the face of the earth. Not to mention that probably, at least half of the married couples who go to that church, or any other church for that matter, are cheating on each other! And they're obligating you to come to church every Sunday to put up with their abuse. Unbelievable!"

"That's not fair, Tony! You're judging these people. You don't even know them." Madonna cried out.

"Madonna, I don't need to get to know them," Tony responded, on the verge of totally losing his temper.

"These people are everywhere. I could throw a rock and hit one of them from here. It's not a secret what kind of character they have. And I don't need to go out of my way to find out how this kind of riffraff operates. I can't help but hear all the gossip that is initiated by these fine, upstanding church people around the company where I'm an executive. I get sick and tired of hearing it. It gets old fast. Did you notice that lady who had that guy cornered in the sanctuary, telling him that she didn't believe he was saved? Why would anyone in their right mind want to associate with individuals hell-bent on making you feel like a bad person? Another thing that I found ridiculous was overhearing that college boy tell a girl that the Lord told him that the two of them were going to get married one day. Then, the girl promptly replied to him: 'Well, the Lord didn't tell me anything about it!' Madonna, I mean, it is to laugh. And did you get a load of that lady who walked up to us in the vestibule, looking me over with that self-righteous, holier-than-thou glare, and saying the word, 'pitiful,' like I wasn't meeting the proper standards to darken the door of her church? And when we were standing in line at the end of the service to greet the Pastor at the front door, and I asked him why he decided to become a minister, he said because the Lord had called him. Then, like some kind of a madman, he took me by the hand and yanked me out of the church. And then, you told him how much you enjoyed his message, and he did the very same thing to you, very rudely tugging you out the door without even thanking you for your kind words. He did it to every single last person who was standing in line to greet him. I read him like a book, a cheap novel. He was acting like a jackass because he thought he was extending some great man of God gesture.

Well, he was behaving like an absolute moron and offending people in the process. And you could tell that Pastor was obviously summing up the assets of everyone in the church. Some people will follow anyone who sets themselves up as a leader! They're all egomaniacs! And these church members don't have the wherewithal to see right through him. They would put any fruitcake in that pulpit to follow! If they acted like they cared about people, it would be different. You're looking at these toxic people through rose-colored glasses, Madonna!"

Tony was becoming more and more enraged as he continued to speak. He was full of anger and totally furious on the topic of church people.

"Tony, please don't let anything keep you from coming back to church next Sunday." Madonna pleaded with a strong emotional appeal.

"You have got to be kidding me, Madonna. I had a miserable experience at that church this morning! Do I need to present my case any further? I have no shortage of evidence to substantiate the proof. They're a bunch of control freaks, Madonna! I could tell that Pastor marks anyone as being evil if they don't agree with him or believe like him. Can't you see that they're just trying to run your life? Those church folks are worse than the thugs out on the street. You need to get away from them before too much damage is done!" Tony adamantly stated.

"Come on, Tony. Give the church one more chance." Madonna sincerely requested as she came closer to Tony.

"There are some nice people there. You're being too harsh."

"No, Madonna! My mind is made up! You can't convince me otherwise. I'm not ever going back there again. I just want to be left alone! Church is a place where you should be inspired and uplifted, not get your life destroyed! Get out of my face with this nonsense!" Tony emphatically insisted as he pushed Madonna forcefully away from himself.

Madonna lost her balance from Tony's powerful shove. She crashed headlong into the sharp edge of a mantle against the wall that displayed a print of Leonardo da Vinci's Mona Lisa painting above it. Madonna landed dramatically on the floor with a horrible-looking gash on her forehead.

Mona Lisa Romano, Tony and Madonna's daughter, came rushing out of her bedroom into the living room, after hearing the entire conversation and screamed, "Mama! Mama!"

In the midst of Mona's screams, Tony went over to Madonna to check her pulse. And with tears in his eyes, he cried out in distressing anguish, "Oh, my God! There's no pulse! She's dead! What am I going to do without her?"

When Mona heard her father say that Madonna was dead, her screams raged totally out of control. Within a few seconds, Abigail Grant, from Apartment 66-A adjacent to the Romano's residence, was banging on the door in response to Mona's outcry.

"Mona! What's wrong? Open the door, Mona!" Abigail shrieked.

As Mona frantically ran to the door to let Abigail inside the Romano's condo, Tony ran into his bedroom, reached into his nightstand drawer, and pulled out a gun.

Mona let Abigail into Apartment 66-B just as Tony came back into the living room. Tony pointed the gun directly at Mona and said, "Stand aside, Abigail. This is none of your affair!"

"Tony, you're pointing that gun at your daughter, your only child!" Abigail declared with utter shock.

"I can't believe that I've lost the love of my life over such a ridiculous, ludicrous issue. It was an accident. I've never hit Madonna in my life. I can't live without her. I wasn't mad at Madonna. I was mad at the topic she and I landed on. And I don't want Mona to endure the hardships of this unkind world without her parents, Abigail!" Tony hollered.

As soon as Tony made it clear that he was going to shoot his own daughter and himself, Abigail immediately grabbed Mona Lisa and yanked the eighteen-year-old girl completely behind her back.

"You're going to have to shoot me first, Tony, before you harm this precious little girl! You're not thinking straight.

You're having a meltdown! Put down the gun, Tony! Put the gun down, and we'll talk." Abigail insisted as calmly as she could.

"There's nothing to talk about." Tony cried out with a contorted look on his face and bloodshot eyes.

"Madonna is gone, and I have absolutely nothing to live for any longer."

With that, Tony put the gun to his head and immediately pulled the trigger, falling to the floor in a splatter of blood.

Abigail had blocked Mona Lisa's view of the shooting.

"Daddy!" Mona screamed out, realizing she may very well have lost both her mother and father in the course of one horrific night.

Both Abigail and Mona Lisa spontaneously went down to the floor and landed on their knees together, closely embracing each other and crying vehemently with quivering lips.

"Oh, Abigail. I feel like the whole world wants me to just lay down and die." Mona wailed.

"That won't happen as long as I'm here, Mona Lisa. I'm going to make sure that you'll be okay. I'll always be here for you." Abigail said in a comforting manner as she gently stroked the back of Mona's head.

2

"Tom McMillan. NYPD, Homicide and Assault Division, Special Victims Unit, 16th Precinct," The detective identified himself to Abigail as he flashed his badge amidst the scuffle of all the activity.

"I'm Abagail Grant. I live at 66-A, the other unit on this floor. I'm a close friend of the Romano family." Abigail stated, still terribly shaken by what had just taken place.

"What's your take on the story here, Ms. Grant?" Tom McMillan got right to the point.

"Well, you're about the last one to ask, Detective McMillan," Abigail retorted.

"Yeah. It took me a while to get up those sixty-six floors," Detective McMillan responded, attempting to add some levity to justify his tardiness. "Exactly what happened here?"

"A senseless tragedy had taken place here tonight, Detective McMillian." Abigail started to explain.

"Tell me about it, Ms. Grant. How did this tragedy begin?" Detective McMillan asked, practically getting his interrogation off the ground in a smart-aleck manner.

"My good friends, Madonna and Tony, got into a bad argument, and Tony accidentally shoved Madonna head first into the edge at the top of that mantle over there and put a serious gash on her forehead," Abigail explained.

"Tony was so grief-stricken that he put a gun to his head and shot himself, but not before he attempted to shoot his daughter, Mona, to prevent her from having to endure living without her parents. He was fully aware that he was going to kill himself after he intended to shoot Mona."

"What stopped him from shooting his daughter, Ms. Grant?" Detective McMillan questioned, with a distinct Bronx accent.

"I quickly grabbed Mona and pulled her in back of me to protect her," Abigail revealed.

"I see. Well, that was extremely courageous of you. And just exactly what were they arguing about, Ms. Grant." Detective McMillan enquired, with as close to a sympathetic tone of voice as he could sincerely muster up.

"Tony had gone to Madonna's church for the first time this morning, and Madonna was trying to persuade Tony to go back again. Tony had no intention of going back, and Madonna kept insisting. Tony got worked up into a fit of rage, and that's when he pushed Madonna." Abigail expounded, wiping tears from her eyes.

"Mona heard everything. She told me the entire story. Tony didn't mean to hurt Madonna, Detective McMillan! He was really in a tizzy, and he was totally out of control!"

"Where is Mona now?" Detective McMillan abruptly asked, appearing concerned about the little girl's welfare.

"She's in her bedroom right now," Abigail indicated.

"And she wasn't physically harmed?" Detective McMillan asked.

"No. Mona wasn't hurt, but of course, she's quite shaken by what's happened!" Abigail said, still totally empathizing with the shock that Mona was feeling.

"Detective McMillan, I don't mean to be premature in making this request. But Mona is without parents, and I am interested in becoming her new guardian. Mona and I know each other quite well. She's won a scholarship to New York University. I know what her personal goals are, and I could be very instrumental in helping her reach those goals."

"Well, I saw the report at the precinct. Mona is eighteen years old. She's legally no longer considered a child. She's an adult who has reached the age of maturity. She can live anywhere in the U.S. she wants." Detective McMillan pointed out.

"I am aware of that, Detective McMillan," Abigail responded.

"I'm just specifying that I would make a perfect guardian for Mona Lisa because I know her all too well. I'm academically inclined as she is, being a doctor of psychology and a clinical psychologist. I've watched her grow for years, and I can financially assist her in reaching the goals she's been striving so hard to achieve. Mona is going through severe trauma right now, Detective

McMillan. She needs to be around someone she knows and trusts. I'd support Mona any way I possibly can."

Tom Millian looked sternly at Abigail. All he could see on her face was absolute sincerity and integrity.

"Danny!" Detective McMillan yelled out loud, knowing for a fact that Danny would already be there. Danny, Detective McMillan's right-hand man, was usually the first or second police detective to show up at crime scenes.

"Yeah, Chief." Danny promptly responded.

"Danny, the wife hit her head on the mantle as a result of a shove from her husband, and Mr. Romano, then, shot himself. Dr. Grant stood in front of Mona Romano to block her from getting shot by her father, who was in a blind rage at the time. He knew he was going to shoot himself, and not being in his right mind, he was attempting to prevent Mona from having to face the future without her parents. Dr. Grant has stated that Mr. Romano was having a serious meltdown after causing his wife's death. Does that cover the read that you have so far, Danny?" Detective McMillian firmly asked.

"That covers it, Chief. And we've already interviewed Mona Romano. That story concurs with the evidence, and we're convinced that's exactly what happened." Danny confirmed.

"Okay. Get Sharon Watson, the case worker at the precinct, on the horn." Detective McMillan ordered.

"I know she's working late because she was telling me about a case that was keeping her there tonight. Tell her we need her expertise up here right away, at my request. Let's see if we can find some solace in the midst of this conundrum."

"Right away, Chief!" Danny urgently said.

It didn't take long for Sharon Watson to arrive at the Romano's residence after receiving Tom McMillan's message. She had familiarized herself with the case as much as possible.

"Sharon, you're just the person I wanted to see." Detective McMillan said with a flair to welcome Sharon Watson.

"I figured out that it has to have something to do with the eighteen-year-old, Tom." Sharon surmised.

"Yes, it does, Sharon." Detective McMillan responded.

"Danny, go get Mona for us. Will you please?"

Danny headed toward Mona's bedroom to get her.

"Sharon, I'd like to introduce you to Dr. Abigail Grant. She's a clinical psychologist. She lives in the condo next to this one. She has been a close friend of Antonio and Madonna Romano for years. And she's seeking to assist Mona in her overall care, future plans, and the cost of her education."

"Well, you may very well be just the right candidate to help Mona through this horrible crisis, Dr. Grant," Sharon stated.

Mona came out of her lavish bedroom with Danny, still sobbing in unbelief over losing her parents. She clutched firmly onto Abigail as the clinical psychologist put her arm around Mona.

"Danny, I want you to check Dr. Grant out for any priors." Detective McMillan directed as Danny acknowledged his request.

"Nothing personal, Ms. Grant. It's just standard procedure."

"I understand perfectly, Detective McMillan," Abigail responded gracefully.

"I don't take it personally at all."

"Abigail saved my life!" Mona blurted out, uncontrollably crying.

"Daddy didn't mean it. He wasn't himself."

It didn't take Mona long to forgive her father.

"Yes, we understand that you and Abigail are very good friends and have known each other for years now. How would you feel about the idea of staying with Abigail for a while until you get your feet on the ground? I believe that she would be a very good influence on you." Sharon sincerely asked Mona.

"Oh, that would be wonderful!" Mona exclaimed with utter exhilaration.

"Abigail is an incredible person!"

Abigail turned toward Mona, "And we could work together on getting you prepared for college at NYU and making good use of the scholarship that you won."

"Have you decided on a major yet, Mona?" Sharon asked.

"I'm going to double major in international affairs and political science," Mona replied very confidently.

"Well, you can do a lot of things with that," Sharon said, genuinely impressed and pleasantly surprised.

"You could even become an attorney if you decide to go to law school."

"Or become involved in foreign policy and diplomacy in some capacity," Mona said, starting to snap back to her amiable self.

"That's most ambitious for a girl your age," Sharon said, somewhat overwhelmed with Mona's purpose in life at such a young age.

"I think your goals are most admirable."

"More power to you, young lady," Detective McMillan added.

"Dr. Grant's record is cleaner than a white Christmas, Chief. There's nothing on her," Danny reported to Detective McMillan.

"Thank you, Danny," Detective McMillan replied.

"Just as I suspected."

"Dr. Grant will be a marvelous mentor for you, Mona. Everyone reflects on their life and wishes they may have had someone like Dr. Grant standing by their side to steer them clear of uncertain perils in the world and help guide them on their journey to success. You're one of the fortunate ones. And there's no telling what unimaginable, unreachable heights you'll attain through all of your endeavors," Sharon eloquently stated with tremendous understanding of the difficult transition Mona was suddenly facing in her life.

"I'll check in on you both from time to time."

"And I will impart whatever wisdom and insight I have to you, Mona, to guide you along the way," Abigail said with great enthusiasm as she pulled Mona Lisa in for a big hug. And Abigail Grant would go on to keep her promise, saving Mona Lisa Romano's life in more ways than one.

3

The family and friends who attended the funeral of Antonio and Madonna Romano were overwhelmed with a sense of utter grief and empathy. There was no condemnation or harsh feelings toward Tony for causing Madonna's death. Everyone knew how crazy Tony was about Madonna and that he would never do anything intentionally to harm his beloved wife. Both Abigail and Mona kept a low profile on Tony pointing a gun at his own daughter.

Detective McMillan, at Abigail's urging, did not allow any authorities to leak that piece of information concerning the news story to the media. Once again, with a sense of urgency, Abigail was protecting Mona. Abigail was regarded as a genuine hero for being there for Mona at this critical moment. And Mona's good heart shined bright as she stood beside Abigail in front of her parent's coffins, with an attitude of forgiveness toward her father. Nevertheless, the entire incident had left Mona spiraling in pain and trauma.

All of Mona's family on both sides were very acquainted with Abigail Grant. And they were all in agreement that Abigail would make a wonderful guardian and tutor for Mona. Abigail's reputation and credentials preceded her. She was well-known and well-liked all over New York City.

And no one could have hand-picked a more solid citizen than Abigail to take care of Mona. Abigail was willing to cover Mona's back to assist her in any way she could.

For Tony's sake, a minister from a church other than Madonna's church was chosen to officiate the funeral.

"So, with all that having been said," the minister, dressed in his holy raiment, narrated in conclusion to his funeral message,

"Let us all with one heart commend Antonio and Madonna Romano to the Lord, the Resurrection and the Life, and pay our sincere tribute to them. We are here today to show our love and support for Tony and Madonna, a couple who will always remain eternally as one. And we are here to render and receive comfort. Today, we are trusting God to give us consolation in this situation as we continue on our own personal journeys. We are going to move beyond our tears. We are going to move beyond our questions. We are going to move beyond the misunderstanding. We are going to move beyond our pain. And we commit all of these matters to you, O, Lord, for it is in your name we pray. Amen."

"Amen." Everyone attending the funeral repeated.

Aunt Rosa, Madonna's sister and Mona Lisa's favorite aunt, grabbed Mona's hand suddenly and said,

"Try not to dwell on this tragedy, Mona. You have your entire life ahead of you, Dear. And you have a very strong support group to back you up, no one stronger than Ms. Abigail here. And we're all going to help you in any way and every way we can to make sure that you're going to be okay. Do you hear me, girl?"

Aunt Rosa reassured, in her sweet Italian manner.

"I hear you, Aunt Rosa." Mona Lisa cheerfully responded, with tears streaming down her face.

"Thank you so much for being there for me."

"I'm always here for you, Mona Lisa. I love you so much. We all love you. You're the most precious girl in the world." Aunt Rosa affirmed.

"I'm not going anywhere. You let me know if you need anything at all, and call me any time you just want to talk. Okay?"

"All right, Aunt Rosa," Mona said in complete agreement, so glad that her favorite aunt was reaching out to her at such a critical moment.

"Everything's going just fine, Dear. You wait and see. You'll see. I believe there's something very special ahead for you!" Aunt Rosa said her parting words to Mona, breaking contact with her niece's hands and going her way with tears rolling down her cheeks as well.

Aunt Rosa was an absolute dynamo. She served as a constant inspiration to the entire family.

Not a single family member failed to take Mona by the hand to render encouragement because they loved her so much. And all of the grief-stricken friends of the family made their way over to Mona as well, sharing kind words and sympathy for her loss. Everyone attending the funeral shook Abigail's hand as well, all acknowledging to the clinical psychologist that the good things they had heard about her were right on target.

432 Park Avenue Apartments — Condo 66-A

"Good morning, sleepyhead," Abigail resounded in a sweet tone of voice.

"I must have dozed off," Mona said, stretching her arms over her head as she laid comfortably in the bed of Abigail's luxurious guest bedroom.

"You didn't even know what hit you after we got home last night. You were completely exhausted. It's quite understandable. You had a long day yesterday," Abigail reasoned.

"It appears that today marks the beginning of me getting prepared for college," Mona casually remarked.

"And I have a great idea. You get dressed, and we'll go down to the 12th floor and have some breakfast at the 432 Park Avenue Restaurant. Perhaps we'll both have an omelet," Abigail suggested with great enthusiasm.

"Oh, that would be perfect, Abigail!" Mona responded.

432 Park Avenue Restaurant - 12th Floor

The entire twelfth floor of the tallest residential building in the Western Hemisphere commands an entire floor for the 432 Park Avenue Restaurant, which includes a 5,000-square-foot terrace. The restaurant is exclusively for the residents who live in the building and their guests. The restaurant provides a dining and entertaining experience unparalleled by any other residential building. The restaurant displays 22-foot cascading chandeliers and 339 hand-blown glass globes that are suspended from polished stainless-steel rods.

432 Park Avenue Apartments Restaurant

Neither Abigail nor Mona were strangers to the restaurant. Abigail ordered the French-style omelet, French toast, yogurt, and seasonal fruit plate with orange juice, and Mona Lisa, in copycat style, made the exact same order.

"Your Aunt Rosa is a very colorful character, Mona. It's quite apparent that she has had a powerful influence on you." Abigail remarked.

"Oh, yes. My Aunt Rosa is a force to be reckoned with, and that's not an understatement or exaggeration. She is always logical, down-to-earth, and pragmatic. People even seek her out for sound advice. She's helped a lot of folks." Mona verified.

"Well, you've been through a lot, Mona. Your Aunt Rosa, myself, and others know that it's caused you to become very vulnerable. This is a very fragile period for you. It's only natural that it will take time for you to sort through the pain of what's happened to you. You have your future ahead in college, and everyone wants you to stay on the right track." Abigail said with genuine concern.

"And I appreciate that people are worried about me. I really do. I'm overwhelmed by everyone's concern. Let me ask you, Abigail, can you arrange it so the Mona Lisa portrait in Mama and Daddy's home can be brought to your condominium?" Mona earnestly implored.

"Sure. I've been meaning to ask you for the longest time about that Mona Lisa picture that's been hanging up in your living room. Does that picture mean anything to you personally?" Abigail asked with genuine curiosity.

A beam of sunshine gleamed across Mona Lisa's face.

"Oh, yes. Mama and Daddy put that picture up together, talking about how the Mona Lisa was the most famous lady on the face of the Earth. And they said that one day I would be just as famous as she is all around the world. Mama and Daddy believed it so much that they named me after the

Mona Lisa." Mona exclaimed cheerfully, reflecting on happier days.

"You know something, Mona Lisa. I don't doubt that one bit." Abigail responded in all sincerity.

"You have so many admirable qualities."

When Abigail made this remark of affirmation, Mona smiled exactly like the Mona Lisa in Leonardo da Vinci's painting. When Abigail keenly observed Mona's smile, the psychologist's reaction was being amazed and startled at the same time.

"You're right, Abigail. I won't get over this pain overnight. It's going to take a long time. I can tell, but I can't allow it to hinder me from achieving my goals. I believe I can make a mark in the world. I know I can do something positive." Mona declared.

"I just graduated from high school, so I need to know the best approach I can take in life."

After Mona spoke, she placed her hands on the table in front of her plate, with her right hand covering her left wrist. Mona also projected a duplicate smile of Leonardo da Vinci's Mona Lisa again. Even young Mona's facial features matched the Mona Lisa portrait. The end of the young Mona Lisa's left lip was slightly tilting upward, just like the prominent lady portrayed in Leonardo da Vinci's most famous painting that's now located at the Louvre Museum in Paris, France. Abigail was eerily taken back by the image before her, unable to control her emerging goosebumps. Abigail also couldn't help but notice that Mona Lisa Romano parted her brown hair down the middle, just as the Mona Lisa parted her hair in the portrait. For that matter, Abigail herself parted her brown hair down the middle as well. Abigail Grant had glimpses of Mona Lisa Romano's resemblance to the Mona Lisa before, but not as vivid as this.

All of Mona Romano's features, her brown hair, brown eyes, and her right hand over her left hand, served to accentuate her similarity to Leonardo da Vinci's Mona Lisa painting.

"Mona, I can share with you very succinctly what your best approach to life should be. Dear, don't look at things as you think they should be. Look at life the way that things actually are in reality. That will make all the difference for you. For example, should we walk around thinking that everyone in the world is a nice person, or is it better to be aware that there are people out there who could potentially wish us harm?" Abigail posed.

"And that's just one aspect of what I'm referring to. And from that vantage point, you can cause changes to make the world as it should be."

Mona repeated Abigail's words under her breath as if she were savoring a thought that she had never pondered before.

"That's powerful, Abigail. I'll never forget that. I promise." Mona Lisa exclaimed.

"When you change the way you see the world, the things you look at change. When your intentions are positive and powerful, and when you search only for the good, then your life transforms into the amazing adventure that it was designed to be." Abigail expounded.

"That's beautiful, Abigail." Mona was engulfed by Abigail's revelation.

Abigail's objective was not to psychoanalyze Mona. Abigail knew Mona's thought processes backward and forward. She knew everything about Mona. But this little girl with so much potential always managed to surprise Abigail.

So, the clinical psychologist's powers of perception where Mona Lisa was concerned were totally confined to discerning the eighteen-year-old's aesthetic value in terms of her beauty, intelligence, elegance, gracefulness, and potential. And Mona had no shortage of any of these qualities. And Abigail's prime directive was to shape Mona's dynamic attributes.

"Abigail, you counsel a lot of famous people, don't you? It kind of explains how you're able to live on Billionaire's Row." Mona asked.

"Yes. A fair share of my clients are well-known celebrities, and I have to admit that they do help to keep my practice thriving." Abigail answered.

"I suppose you can't really say who some of these superstars may be, huh?" Mona asked, already knowing the answer.

"That's right. I think you know that would be a betrayal of trust and confidence." Abigail confirmed.

"It's hard to believe that superstars have problems so serious that they need to see a clinical psychologist," Mona said.

"Mona, if you knew some of the difficulties that these famous people face, it would terrify you," Abigail remarked in all seriousness.

"Wow! You'd think with all the money and fame that they have, they wouldn't have a care in the world. Seems like they would be on Easy Street," Mona retorted.

"If you only knew!" Abigail responded.

"It appears that fame is not all that it's cracked up to be. Fame and fortune are not all glamor."

"Still, at the same time, it has to be thrilling to get to know some of these people," Mona pointed out.

"Oh, yes. I regard many of them as good friends, and I suppose there are some who would say the same thing about me. They certainly aren't shy about referring other celebrities to me," Abigail mentioned humbly.

"You've helped a lot of people, Abigail. And people will never forget you for it," Mona sweetly said.

"And how about you, Mona? Where do you see yourself after you've completed your education? Become an attorney, work for a government agency or political organization, go into broadcast journalism specializing in international affairs, international banking and business, perhaps connect forces with a congressional office or executive department, do some university teaching or research, join the Peace Corp, the State Department, or the United States Department of Defense? The possibilities are endless for you. Where do you see yourself? Luck is what happens when preparation meets opportunity, you know," Abigail enquired.

"Well, I must say, you certainly have narrowed down the options quite accurately. I'd like to get into an arena where there's some kind of negotiating taking place. It sure would be nice to be a part of bringing peace to this world," Mona quickly responded.

"Well, there's one thing I know about negotiating," Abigail said.

"What's that?" Mona asked, genuinely curious.

"In any negotiation, there will always be pressure on both sides of the table, not just yours," Abigail responded with a look of confidence.

"We live in a world where misunderstanding and misinterpretation oftentimes lead to conflict."

Mona reacted with her vintage, trademark smile.

"That's so true, it's funny, Abigail," Mona blurted out.

"There goes that Mona Lisa smile of yours again that I've come to love," Abigail said affectionately.

"Thank you, Abigail. It just seems that no matter what you do in life, everyone expects you to be perfect." Mona said in a despondent way.

"We're not intended to be perfect, Mona. Whoever's perfect belongs in a museum," Abigail sited.

This time, Abigail made Mona burst out with laughter.

"That's hilarious!" Mona cried out with tickled ribs.

"There's a big difference between perfectionism and simply doing a good job. Perfectionism implies that you can't make any mistakes. That's ridiculous. We learn from our mistakes," Abigail insisted.

"Well, the objective is to prosper and live happily. There ought to be a constitution to that effect. That constitution should state that no person, group of persons, or government may initiate force, threat of force, or fraud against any individual's self or property. Securing the rights of life, liberty, and the pursuit of happiness in order to form a more perfect Union would serve to compliment this constitution, of course. At least it's stated in the United States Declaration of Independence," Mona stated out of indignation.

"In fact, international affairs and world order should work toward that end for all nations."

"My goodness. You're already sounding just like a stateswoman and the all-American girl!" Abigail declared.

"I think I would have an epiphany of my destiny if it weren't for some of my bad memories," Mona confided to the psychologist, almost sounding depressed.

"Mona, your negative memories may appear to be very powerful, but they can benefit you as much as positive memories because they will open you to new experiences. The pain associated with bad memories can detour you away from adverse occurrences in the future, serving as red flags based on past occurrences. Negative memories prompt us to practice self-compassion, stand back to take an objective look at the situation, take a moment to sense our instincts and feelings, and consider whether or not we should seek out advice. It is imprudent to ignore negative emotions because these uncomfortable feelings should be regarded as opportunities to learn. Negative emotions are not obstacles because the best days of your life are ahead of you. Bad memories confirm to us that suffering makes us more resilient and better able to endure hardships," Abigail rendered.

"And rejection from people is something that hurts the person who's doing the rejecting, which leaves them with scars. Because after a while, you realize that the problem does not lie with yourself, but with the person doing all of the rejecting."

Mona couldn't believe her ears. She knew that Abigail was pouring her psychological guts out to support her.

"Wow! You really are a psychologist. How much do I owe you for sharing all of this keen awareness?" Mona said most sincerely, with her mouth hanging open.

"No charge for you, Mona," Abigail replied very lovingly and cheerfully.

"Just for you, it's on the house."

In a big way, Abigail was fighting for Mona's life. The tragedy and trauma of her mother and father's deaths were fresh, and Abigail possessed the tools to keep Mona proceeding in the proper direction. But it would be up to Mona to comprehend and effectively apply what Abigail was attempting to convey to her. Fortunately, Mona was a pretty quick study. Abigail was in luck. In Mona Lisa Romano, she had a very bright protégé to enlighten. Yet there would be moments when it was Mona illuminating Abigail.

"And so far as your career is concerned, especially in regard to your field of endeavor," Abigail added.

"Don't ever forget that you have power over your mind, but not external events. You cannot control what other people do. And many times, you can't control circumstances. But you have total control over achieving your own goals. So, despite any circumstances we may find ourselves in, we can always give an impeccable performance."

"And it's especially true of the power-hungry people all around us. It's a challenge ignoring them and achieving our goals from day to day," Mona responded in despair.

"Because once people acquire power, they will do anything and everything they possibly can to hold on to it," Abigail said.

"Well, the one thing everyone says, whether they're young or old, is that life is short," Mona said.

"Life's biggest tragedy is that we grow old too soon and become wise too late," Abigail interjected.

"But at the same time, anyone who can see beauty will never grow old. Mona, I'm going to share something with you that I never want you to forget, because I believe you're going to be influencing many people in the future: People will forget what you said. They will forget what you did. But they will never forget how you made them feel. And what we do for the people who matter to us will echo in eternity."

As Abigail and Mona made their way to the elevator to get back to the sixty-sixth floor of the 432 Park Avenue Condominium Apartments, Mona turned to Abigail and said, "Abigail, for someone as contemporary, accomplished, and affluent as yourself, you certainly are down to Earth at the same time."

"I've just always been practical, straightforward, and easy to relate to. I care about the world, and I work to improve it," Abigail responded in a congenial manner.

4

Central Park New York, New York

Central Park, New York City

Central Park is an urban park between the Upper West Side and Upper East Side neighborhoods of Manhattan in New York City that has been described as the very first landscaped park in the United States. It is the fifth largest park in New York City, containing 843 acres. Central Park is the most visited urban park in the United States. It was created between 1857 to 1876. The main attractions of the park include the Jacqueline Kennedy Onassis Reservoir, Central Park Carousel, Central Park Zoo, Central Park Mall, the Delacorte Theater, Shakespeare in the Park, and many others.

Central Park has 21 children's playgrounds (including the Diana Ross Playground), 26 baseball fields, 2 ice skating rinks, 12 tennis courts, and an outdoor swimming pool. Central Park is patrolled by its own New York City Police Department precinct, the NYPD Central Park Precinct (CPP). In total, over 20,000 people helped construct Central Park, which was difficult because of the generally rocky and swampy landscape that had initially existed. Central Park is surrounded by a 29,025-foot-long stone wall and accessed by 20 named gates. The park contains around 9,500 benches in three different styles. Central Park has been the site of musical concerts and theater productions almost since its inception.

Since the mid-20th century, Central Park has had a reputation for being a very dangerous place, especially after dark. Central Park's size, cultural position, and landscape design have served as a model for many urban parks. A New York City icon, Central Park is the most filmed location in the world. Many movies have been produced in Central Park (and Times Square) for both dramatic and romantic movie shooting scenes. Central Park has been designated as a National Historic Landmark since 1963.

The dark and precarious side of Central Park did not phase Abigail Grant one bit. In comparison, she had experienced far too many joyful moments at the park to be detoured by any risk of danger. She knew how to stay on the park's safe side. Abigail had embarked on a new career of creating positive, healthy diversions for Mona Lisa to keep her mind off the pain of having so abruptly and horrifically lost her parents, or at least channeling Mona's pain into focusing on more constructive venues. And Central Park to Abigail Grant embodied all the possibilities of accomplishing that very endeavor.

Abigail took Mona to the Great Lawn at Central Park to be entertained by the New York Philharmonic Orchestra, one of the most important symphonic ensembles in the United States, appearing more than 6,000 times at Carnegie Hall. Abigail also wanted to give Mona Lisa exposure to Shakespeare in the Park, a theatrical program that stages productions of Shakespearean plays at the Delacorte Theater, of course, located in New York City's Central Park. Abigail shared all her favorite sites of Central Park to the sheer great delight of Mona Lisa Romano.

But on one very special day that summer before Mona would embark on her freshman year at New York University, better known as NYU, the two Central Park explorers also went to New York's largest museum, the Metropolitan Museum of Art (The Met), located on the east side of Central Park, where Leonardo da Vinci's original painting of the Mona Lisa was displayed, after being brought to the United States by the wife of the 35th President of America. Jacqueline Bouvier Kennedy's charming influence on the people of France, resulting from the impact of her visit to the country with President Kennedy in 1961 made it possible for the Mona Lisa to be lent to the United States by the Republic of France and exhibited first at the National Gallery of Art in Washington, D.C., and then at the New York Metropolitan Museum of Art in Central Park. It was on the final day of their pilgrimage to France that John F. Kennedy stated at the Palais de Chaillot in Paris: "I am the man who accompanied Jacqueline Kenndy to Paris, and I've enjoyed it." Jackie's powerful impact in France even overshadowed the popularity of the President of the United States, and JFK knew it. Courtesy of Jackie's allure, over one million people were able to clamor to see the Mona Lisa at the Metropolitan Museum of Art during the portrait's stay.

JFK, Jacqueline Kennedy And The Mona Lisa

The Metropolitan Museum Of Art — The Met

And now, Abigail Grant and Mona Lisa Romano stood directly in front of the very spot where the Mona Lisa painting had once been exhibited in 1963, with a red curtain background. They both stood there solemnly, picturing in their minds how prominent the Mona Lisa portrait must have looked when it had been displayed at The Met so long ago. It wasn't long before Abigail and Mona simultaneously began to sense a distinct, overwhelming feeling of buoyancy.

A joyful presence suddenly surrounded them both. A clearly definite sensation of exuberance completely overtook Abigail and Mona's senses.

Mona Lisa At The Met In New York City In 1963

"I can't explain it, but all of a sudden, I've never felt so cheerful and optimistic in my life!" Abigail exclaimed.

"I know why. The Mona Lisa's portrait may not be here now, but her presence remains from the period when the painting was here in 1963," Mona mysteriously responded.

Abigail was startled and even somewhat spooked by Mona's confident demeanor.

"Well, Mona. I'm so overwhelmed by whatever is happening right now that I will gladly hear your take on what may be causing this!" Abigail entreated.

"Her picture doesn't even need to be here now. What's happening is that her portrait was here at one time. She leaves her presence behind wherever she goes. You and I are present now at a very special place," Mona clarified.

"I'll say!" Abigail remarked, curious and shocked, that any hidden meaning of the phenomenon did not come as any surprise to Mona. "It's like an awakening!"

"Now, you're getting it," Mona said, looking directly at Abigail with her big, brown eyes, projecting an air of wisdom beyond her years.

Abigail resigned not to pursue any further line of questioning. She didn't need any more convincing that what was taking place was absolutely real. The joy was so intense that she could cut it with a knife. But Mona's nonchalance to the situation was creating an element of eeriness. Mona was referring to the Mona Lisa as if she had known her all her life.

Abigail simply could not understand how Mona could possibly be reacting so lightly and casually to something so incredibly out of the ordinary. Mona acted like it was an event that took place every day of the week.

Abigail and Mona remained there, absorbing the moment at what they both considered to be a sacred site, for an undetermined amount of time before making their way back to the great outdoors of Central Park. Even though the priceless portrait was not present at the time of their visit together, it seemed more than poetic for Abigail to take Mona to the very place where the original Mona Lisa painting was once proudly exhibited and admired by so many people.

In the delightful process, Mona became, equally as much as Abigail, a connoisseur of the fine arts. After leaving the Metropolitan Museum of Art that day, Abigail and Mona strolled through Central Park, whose entire park length could be covered in fifty minutes of walking at a moderate pace. It seemed only fitting, after their wonderful experience at The Met, for them to have yet another engaging conversation. Abigail was good about not allowing themselves to land on deep topics too often. She could turn it on wherever she desired and then turn it right back off again. Abigail didn't want the heavy topics to get old. She didn't want to wear it out. So, she approached it all in great moderation, spoon-feeding Mona. But Abigail knew that she had much to share with her protégé to benefit, enhance, and enrich her young life. The attractive, thirty-four-year-old Abigail Grant was making an impression on the naïve Mona Lisa Romano in leaps and bounds.

Whether Mona Lisa realized it or not, Abigail was determined to catch Mona at every turn to prevent her from succumbing to her own personal pain, with the end result of her becoming a full-time, eighteen-year-old party girl trying to drown her sorrows. Abigail knew Mona had too much potential to throw her life away or live it frivolously without meaning. And Abigail was privy to just the right tools to tweak Mona's misfortunes into stepping stones rather than hindrances. And Abigail worked her magic quite gracefully, a mannerism that carried over into every aspect of her life.

"Well, I believe David Letterman said it best in regard to us: 'We've been having more fun than human beings are allowed to have.'" Abigail jested as she and Mona walked through Central Park together on a beautiful, perfectly blue sky, sunny day after recently enjoying the main event of visiting The Met and basking in the presence of the Mona Lisa.

"I'll say!" Mona joyously concurred, sharing her side of the story. "We've been having a whirlwind of fun this summer."

Abigail and Mona gravitated to a park bench to rest their feet.

"I somehow manage to keep up with your boundless energy, Mona," Abigail noted.

"You're the youngest person in spirit that I know, Abigail. I'm the one keeping up with you," Mona said, just for the record.

"Mona, the secret of genius is to carry the spirit of the child into old age, which simply means never losing your enthusiasm," Abigail said.

"And another aspect of this secret is to live in the present moment at any given second. Don't dwell in the past. Make peace with the past so it doesn't adversely affect your present moment, despite how traumatic some of the memories of our past may be. Allow the negative experiences of your past to serve as stepping stones and catalysts that teach you how not to be distracted away from your personal goals. And do not daydream about the future. It will come in due time. Concentrate the mind on the present moment. When you observe an hourglass in motion, it's quite apparent that the law of physics will not allow anyone to force the sand to go through the hourglass any faster than it naturally flows. The past is merely the sand below that has already sifted through the hourglass, representing all the previous occurrences of our lives that cannot possibly be changed or altered. Our best recourse is to proceed joyfully in the present moment. The small aperture at the center of the hourglass represents the passing moment of Now when time is energized with the significance of life. This is the secret of remaining eternally young."

Mona soaked up Abigail's every word like water into a sponge. Mona Lisa had already surmised a long time ago that Abigail was very gifted.

"So, the ticket is not to look back because we're not heading in that direction," Mona said to summarize.

"That's exactly right," Abigail said.

"Everything else has either passed or is unknown. The past is history, and the future is a mystery. Living in the present allows you more control over what will happen. We live only for Now. The harder a person's past may have been, the more beautiful their future will be. Dwelling on the past causes us to worry. And most of the stuff we worry about never happens. An overactive imagination will cause us to suffer more than anything in reality could throw our way. And the pain that we feel today from what's happened in the past will serve to be the strength we will feel tomorrow. The storms of life are not designed to disrupt our lives. They come to clear our path to the future. We use some of the pieces of the past to snap the entire superpuzzle together."

"That sounds like something that requires a certain degree of discipline." Mona determined.

"Yes," Abigail affirmed.

"And the moment we let go of our discipline is the very moment when we give up on ourselves. Discipline is like the river that cuts through a rock, not necessarily because of its power alone but because of its persistence as well. Discipline makes today hard but tomorrow easier. Excuses of the past make today easier, but tomorrow harder." Abigail added.

"Life's most significant achievements often emerge from the depths of past adversity. Even mistakes we make are stepping stones to learn from so that we may move forward. Mistakes do not need to be stumbling blocks."

"It sounds like the only real mistake is the one which we learn nothing from." Mona pointed out.

"Sometimes you win, Mona. Sometimes, you learn." Abigail responded with a glowing smile, so very proud of Mona Lisa's remark.

"If you believe the past can be used to your advantage, you will see opportunities. If you believe it won't work to your benefit, you will see obstacles. Then, you can let go of what was, have faith in what will be, and accept what really is. Then, you're capable of being obsessed with becoming the best version of yourself that you can be. Your future needs you. Your past doesn't. Detachment from your past is better than clinging to your past. We fall. We break. We fail. But then, we rise. We heal. We overcome. Every high and low, every joy and sorrow, is an integral part of our narrative."

"In other words," Mona interjected, "Don't let yesterday take up too much of today, even if people try to hold your past against you."

Once again, Abigail could not help but delight in Mona Lisa's brilliant mind.

"One day, Mona Lisa, the people that didn't even believe in you will tell everyone about the day when they first met you." Abigail asserted, bragging on her Mona Lisa.

"The truth of the matter is that everyone, in some way or another, is going to hurt you. You just have to find the special ones worth suffering for. Turn your wounds into wisdom. An eagle uses the storm to soar to unimaginable heights. Train your mind to be stronger than your emotions. Problems are not stop signs. They are guidelines. So far as living in the Now, I think Henry David Thoreau said it best when he expressed, 'I learned this, at least by my experiment: If one advances confidently in the direction of his or her dreams, and endeavors to live the life which he or she has imagined, that person will meet with a success unexpected in common hours. This world is but a canvas to the imagination.'"

"That's incredible, Abigail!" Mona Lisa declared.

"Henry David Thoreau. He graduated from Harvard University just like you, didn't he?"

"Yes, Mona, he certainly did," Abigail firmly verified.

"And even though he didn't become a captain of industry or a United States President like so many other Harvard graduates, he is one of my genuine heroes, and he was a genius. He was a man who had a keen understanding of the power of nature. And even more than that, he was well aware of nature's overwhelming affect upon humanity. And he believed that one glorious day, nature would have her way in the affairs of mankind in every way imaginable. Thoreau participated with nature by cherishing the simple joys of life. He also believed the more you face challenges, the less you fear them. He knew that difficulties are designed to strengthen the mind. He didn't seek to have events happen as he wished. He resolved to allow events to occur exactly as they happened. And as a result, all was well with Henry David Thoreau. He knew that we only lose what we cling to. Through detachment, he learned to navigate the seas, or in his case, Walden's Pond.

Detachment taught him to fully engage in life through nature. He always saw beauty in the challenges that life threw his way. He recognized difficulties as occasions for growth to shape our lives."

"My goodness. Henry David Thoreau is rapidly becoming one of my favorite heroes, too." Mona Lisa concurred.

"Thoreau used nature to better understand the world as a whole. Both Henry David Thoreau and Ralph Waldo Emerson believed that the people of the world could achieve oneness with nature. This, of course, would all be in an effort to save humanity from itself." Abigail astutely commented.

"Well, for someone like myself pursuing a career in international affairs, you know that's music to my ears," Mona said with genuine glee.

Just as much as the more experienced in life Sean McGuire (a psychologist played by Robin Williams) imparted his insight in somewhat rough man-to-man overtones with the not-so-serious-about-life Will Hunting (a 20-year-old mathematical genius played by Matt Damon) in the famous conversation scene they had together at Boston Public Garden on a park bench (which later became a shrine) in the movie, "Good Will Hunting" (which won two Academy Awards and received nominations in nine categories), Dr. Abigail Grant too was fighting for the future of her young, tender protégé, Mona Lisa Romano. As qualified mentors, both Sean McGuire and Abigail Grant's desire, out of protection and promotion, through a heart-to-heart park bench talk, was to inspire their apprentices to make sound decisions, to resolve past conflicts, to think for themselves, and to make their own path clear through love and happiness. Perhaps a park bench, even more than a couch, is a better therapeutic prop. A park, Central Park, in this case, is a more effective setting than an office for a heartfelt conversation.

"When we cannot change situations, we are challenged to change ourselves," Abigail resumed.

"Because then, and precisely then, we are called upon ourselves to demonstrate our unique human potential, which is to turn a predicament into an achievement, that is, a human accomplishment, and convert a tragedy into a triumph. Whenever we're confronted with an unchangeable fate in a situation, even then, there remains the highest level of meaning and potential to both realize and find fulfillment."

"It's just like Mama used to always say: "All things work together for good." Mona fondly reminisced.

"I could not have said it better, Mona Lisa," Abigail responded.

"Life is not a matter of escaping the reality of pain, but pursuing meaning and navigating with a sense of purpose. Even in the darkest night of the soul, stars of meaning and purpose can shine brightly. Life, in all its complexity, is meaningful. Acceptance is not passive resignation. It's an active conscious choice to embrace life as it truly is, not as we think it should be. In every unexpected twist in life lies the opportunity to grow, to learn, and to come closer to our authentic purpose. May we find total acceptance where once there were pockets of resistance. Through this process, we will not only discover serenity but also a deeper, more profound connection with the intricate, beautiful dance that is life. Rather than emotionally reacting to our own biases and expectations, we step back long enough to observe our own thoughts. Then, we are able to more clearly understand what is actually within our control and what is not. And then, we can take a course of action to leverage that control by, first of all, changing ourselves and afterward, if possible, changing the world around us for the better."

"So, our own misconceptions can prevent us from realizing our authentic purpose in life. And resistance to accept people and things in the world as they are in reality will cause serious problems," Mona summarized.

"Mona, when we resist the actual reality of the people and world around us," Abigail continued without skipping a beat, "choosing rather to project our own expectation of how the world should be, we are often met with a certain degree of internal resistance. This sort of resistance has caused many people to suffer. And the greater the difference between actual reality and our own expectation of how everyone and everything should be, the greater the resistance and, therefore, the greater the suffering. It is the ability to see things around us clearly that will give us the capability to correctly interpret people and situations. We find ourselves by refusing to view through the blinding lens of our own preconceptions. We cannot always choose our external circumstances. But we can always choose how we respond to them," Abigail said as she took Mona's hand and looked straight into her eyes.

"You have power over your mind, not outside events. Focus on what you can control, and let go of what you cannot control. Mastering yourself is true power. This is why some of the best times in your life are yet to come. All those seeking tranquility must do what is essential, focusing on what is most important and what truly matters. By doing this, we achieve the fulfillment we need to enrich the quality of our lives. We approach our chosen tasks with greater precision and care. This leads to more time that can be devoted to the quiet, tranquil moments. Embrace life's inevitable losses, responding with composure and integrity in the face of adversity. And the ability to determine your own thoughts is the greatest power of all in mastering yourself. If you set your mind on what you can control, it will always happen the way you imagine it. It's the most feasible way to make the best of a bad situation that you have no control over. No one can determine your state of mind. When we are in control of ourselves, we maintain our dignity and integrity, not allowing ourselves to be manipulated by exterior circumstances, gossip, rumors, and many petty matters that are not in our power. We will find calm in the midst of the chaos when we keep our minds on the right things. We have an incredible understanding of the work that needs to be performed when we have power of control over ourselves."

"I think I'm beginning to get what you're conveying, Abigail." Mona declared.

"And it all is quite imperative in our ever-changing world."

"Change is the one thing we can all count on," Abigail said.

"Changes are always around the next corner. And in response to these changes, it is always worth it to approach them all by doing our very best. To refuse to allow our thoughts to be filled with calamity will make way for clear personal values, goals, and interests. Choosing the essentials in our lives will make this possible. We must control our attitudes, emotions, and opinions. Not allowing ourselves to be manipulated by circumstances outside of our control does not mean being passive. Being in control means you know how to react appropriately, even in the worst of circumstances that frustrate or anger you. We can't control the will of anyone but ourselves. If we are in control, we will adopt an upbeat outlook as we go forward. In other words, ignore all the rest and concentrate on the things that you can directly influence. As quickly as possible, distinguish clearly between the things you can't control and the things you can. Have no worries over things you have absolutely no control over. We can't control everything that happens to us. But we can control how we respond to these matters. It is imperative to make these distinctions. The power to remain mentally unshaken and emotionally resilient lies within us. This engagement will make more meaningful, joyful, quality moments possible. You are an important player participating in a play. It's your job to render a great performance in the part that you have been chosen to perform, becoming the master of yourself as only you can do. You are the only one who can reach your goals, not anyone else. We need to care about our own opinion of ourselves more than other people's opinions about us. You are the only one who has total control over your attitudes, actions, reactions, thoughts, and points of view."

"And there appears to be so many points of view out there in the world, Abigail," Mona responded.

"I went to church a lot with Mama. But I also had a million conversations with Daddy as well. I learned a lot from both of them. Daddy used to talk about how the church people never agreed about anything. And I'm inclined to agree with him because I saw them argue many times in church, especially over doctrinal matters. I knew there was something wrong with it, too. There are over 2,000 churches of many various denominations just in New York City alone, and it's all based on division, not unity. Daddy was right when he said that a lot of these people think like they're from another planet. He would talk about how difficult it is to get a straight answer out of anyone, including medical, legal, and clergy experts. He would always say, 'If you expect nothing from anyone, then you'll never be disappointed.' On the other hand, Mama would always say, 'To be interesting, be interested in others.' Perhaps they're both right. I used to laugh when Daddy told me, 'Be careful who you trust. Salt and sugar look the same.' Based on the way I hear them talk, most church people are only interested in television shows, movies, and books that involve murder, mayhem, vampires, werewolves, and so forth. They don't care about things that are wholesome. I suppose they consider what is honorable to be boring. You would expect more from these people because they should have understanding. But they have no empathy. And they, certainly, have no compassion. Why is there no empathy or compassion among people who claim to be the salt of the earth and representatives of God? Many unsuspecting, innocent, well-intending families come to church for the first time seeking refuge and solace and become the target of idle gossip perpetrated by two-faced individuals. All of these poor people, who are trying to find an oasis, experience condemnation and put-downs because the church members don't think these nice people are good enough to be part of their church. I've witnessed it, Abigail."

"I know, Mona. A lot of those church people are determined to choke all the joy out of life," Abigail agreed.

"I've counseled many, many clients whose lives have been absolutely devastated and demoralized by making the unfortunate mistake of going to the wrong church. Some of them will never be the same again because they were hurt so badly. I've heard my fair share of cruel stories. I've witnessed the atrocities firsthand, too. It requires a good deal of fortitude to not be overwhelmed. Many church members create horrible problems in the church and are very quick to blame others for the problems they've created. It's called projection. And, of course, they do lack compassion in a place where compassion should be in abundance. Unfortunately, many unaware, good-hearted people find out too late just how things really are in this kind of church. After the damage is done, there are many times when the hurt is irreparable. This is a prime example of what happens when people put their trust in other individuals who are not worthy to be trusted. There is no style to many of these church members, and there is no substance or class. They do not forgive, and they do not forget. They quote verses like, 'Confess your faults one to another' and 'Bear one another's burdens,' and then they use your personal information against you. They blab that confidential information all over the church. They even use details that they derive from prayer requests and personal testimonies. The ministers have no sense of confidentiality either where it concerns people's private lives. Many times, they're the worst ones of all. A lot of church pastors let their power go to their heads. All the backslapping from the church members manages to turn the pastor into a monster. They use the Bible as a tool to control the masses. These kinds of pastors only cause harm to other individuals. If they do you a favor, they will hold it over your head forever. They will destroy other people's lives and expect these poor souls to thank them for it. I had mentioned that they were choking the joy out of life. The terrifying aspect of it is that they seem to do it intentionally! These are all harsh lessons to learn. I'm afraid that there are some fates even worse than death. The ticket is to not allow them to do it. Cut them off silently, without reacting. If your absence doesn't affect them, then your presence never mattered. Of course, not everyone who goes to church is like this sort of person. That's too much of a generalization. But unfortunately, many crazies do not stop at the church door. There are some real villains who manage to gain admittance. And these kinds of people really do intentionally approach vulnerable souls and get their jollies out of destroying their lives. There are even church leaders in high positions who are not in their right mind. It's a horrible dilemma to find yourself seeking truth in the wrong place. In the first century, bystanders would proclaim about religious people, 'See how they love one another.' Today, these same observers of church members would declare in disgust, 'See how they fight one another.' The worst form of evil imaginable comes to you in the name of good, Mona."

It was all too apparent that Abigail's advice was rendered in a very strategic fashion to protect Mona from harmful sources that blindside innocent people unmercifully without warning. Abigail knew exactly what she was doing.

"Life honestly is too short for all of us to not show love," Mona said empathetically. "The prospect of death should remind us to live every day to the fullest. None of us know when the end may come. So, if we have not love, we have nothing."

"A lot of people want to go to heaven, Mona Lisa," Abigail retorted, "but they don't want to die."

"Mama had a favorite Bible verse that she used to recite to me all the time. She said it so often to me that I know it by heart. The verse is II Peter 1:4: 'Whereby are given unto us exceeding great and precious promises: That by these you might be partakers of the divine nature, having escaped the corruption that is in this world through lust.' Ideally, I love this verse that Mama shared with me. And of course, becoming a partaker of the divine nature means partaking of a nature more powerful than our own as human beings. But I'm inclined to agree with Daddy that no one on Earth appears to be doing that, Abigail. Do you know why?" Mona Lisa sincerely enquired.

Abigail bowed her head for a few seconds in deep contemplation and responded with a sigh, "It's because nobody wants it, Mona. We all have a human nature that causes us to think more about what we want for ourselves than what's best for all concerned. And our nature has such a grip on us that we don't even want to think in terms of partaking of a divine nature. It's a sad, pitiful state of affairs. The human race may have an answer to all of our difficulties that is right under our nose, and none of us want it."

"Abigail, it is amazing that you are objective enough to give me that kind of an answer!" Mona exclaimed.

"I've just been around the block a little bit, Mona Lisa," Abigail explained. "Very kind of you to say so. Of course, kindness is a virtue that you have no shortage of."

"Kindness is the language that the deaf can hear and the blind can see," Mona said in true, top form.

"And there certainly is a lot to be said about how kindness is the quickest route to manifesting happiness." Abigail expounded. "We should always do everything out of kindness and fairness. I'm confident that the genuine kindness you possess, Mona Lisa, will cause you to remain true to your designated path of destiny. Because I can vividly see that your kindness causes you to not be angry with the world, but compassionate and understanding toward it. Your natural, disarming charm will aid you in adhering to your bigger plan, aiming for goodness in all that you do, and discarding everything that is considered random. I predict, Mona, that the combination of your kindness, charm, patience, and negotiating skills will blend quite effectively in your work toward a better community. There's no telling how large that community may encompass. But I do know it will all be a part of the universe's design. Your ability to be considerate of others will serve to bring you sound reasoning and rationale. And that reason will effortlessly navigate you through all of your challenges. Your pragmatic thinking, understanding, and peace of mind will flow smoothly to all other people concerned. You'll figure out how to take any obstacle and use it to your advantage. And you'll discover that what happens to you does not define you, but your interpretation of these things is what characterizes you. And the resulting appeal of your powerful statements and interactions will be irresistible."

"It is quite apparent that effectively grasping these principles would bring about a tremendous degree of happiness, individually, and completeness." Mona surmised.

Abigail never ceased to be taken back from time to time by the sharpness of Mona Lisa's mind.

"We discover happiness when we join the dance of life's ever-changing rhythms, Mona," Abigail announced with elation. "We all find peace from doing the right things in life. This is what brings about true balance and order. This is what contributes to everything becoming organized so we may live in harmony. We find joy by doing good for others. And I know you well enough to realize that this goal is your ultimate objective. This is where your life's journey is leading you. You're a thoughtful human being, and that in and of itself will bring you happiness. I see a lot of goodness in you, and before long, many other people will notice your source of goodness as well. And we'll end this conversation today on a cheerful note of happiness. And what better topic to close with, because I believe that you are going to be instrumental in bringing happiness to many people in the future. Your father was involved in international affairs through the import/export business, providing you with an understanding of how changes in foreign policies affect the world's economy, and your mother was an international affairs attorney with a very prestigious law firm, giving you a tremendous amount of insight into the legalities of international affairs. You have expressed a sincere desire to help the world through the venue of negotiating in regard to international affairs. And I know that you are going to be a force to be reckoned with. International affairs is in your genes. It's a field of endeavor that you were born to pursue. I'm convinced of that. And through the process of accomplishing your worthwhile goals, you are going to learn to rest in the fact that you don't need anyone's permission to be happy. Life is a mystery to be experienced, but many people succumb to the undercurrent of insecurity due to the seeming impermanence of life. You will not become one of these victims. We must realize that discernment and self-introspection help us to access pertinent wisdom and guidance. Proper decisions must be made and exerted by the people who want to live a happy life. And for all concerned, happiness is what it's all about. This is the race, and these are the Olympic games, and there is no more time to waste."

Both Abigail and Mona Lisa walked away from that park bench in Central Park with a definite feeling that the conversation they had just engaged in together on that day was meant to be. It was a special moment for these two ladies, who glowed with renewed vigor and radiance. The bond of their relationship was now officially eternal. And there was no denying that their visitation just prior to the very place where the Mona Lisa's original portrait had once been displayed played a major role in contributing to the inspiration of their timeless discussion. It more than appeared that the spirit of the Mona Lisa herself had intervened on Abigail and Mona's behalf.

5

At Mona Lisa's request, Abigail salvaged the Mona Lisa portrait that once hung over the mantle at the Romano's residence of their 432 Park Avenue 66-B condominium. Abigail chose to display the painting in front of her living room sofa, where it could be comfortably admired.

The Mona Lisa is the most famous, most expensive, and most mysterious picture in the world. It is estimated to be worth close to a billion dollars. Each year, millions of people flock to visit the portrait at the Louvre Museum in Paris, France, where it can be viewed behind an enclosed armored, bulletproof, earthquake-shatterproof glass case.

The Mona Lisa has remained a shining star for centuries among all of Leonardo da Vinci's works of art. The secrets of the Mona Lisa make her special, right down to her enigmatic, mysterious, elusive, and captivating smile. Many people find the Mona Lisa to represent the most supreme, formidable femme fatale of all time, possessing ideal beauty. She was painted by the greatest genius of all time, Leonardo da Vinci, the artist, scientist, and inventor. The dark clothing that she's wearing and the veil over her hair give the impression that she is in mourning. But her teasing smile subtly offsets the expression of her melancholy face. Her gaze appears to wander off. Yet her eyes always meet viewers as they move from one side of the room to the other where she is displayed. She seems to carefully follow us with her eyes wherever we go, hence the Mona Lisa effect.

The Mona Lisa is considered to be the greatest artistic masterpiece of all time. The Mona Lisa's smile conveys the impression that she knows something that we don't. This is why she has mesmerized so many people for so long. The portrait is a work of art that embodies the height of the Renaissance. She continues to baffle and fascinate us. She is a global phenomenon, recognized and revered by people from all backgrounds and walks of life. Her beguiling smile and serene gaze create a mystique that serves to amplify her allure, magnetically drawing observers from all over the world.

This timeless portrait is a unique combination of art, mystery, and history. Each mystical piece of the superpuzzle that we uncover makes the Mona Lisa even more intriguing. She is a hypnotic reflection of life. To this day, the Mona Lisa shrouded in perplexity and intrigue, has never stopped dazzling the perspective of art lovers. Her intimate smile hints that she is prepared to share her secrets with humanity concerning the order of nature. The complex dimensions of the Mona Lisa require much further explanation. She is the subject of endless speculations. It's as if she desires to awaken our imagination if only we would allow our senses to reciprocate appropriately. Obviously, there is more to the Mona Lisa than meets the eye.

Mona Lisa Romano became a permanent fixture at Dr. Abigail Grant's condominium. Abigail was more than happy to assist Mona with any and all expenses that were not covered by her scholarship to New York University. Abigail, being a keen academic herself, was absolutely dazzled by Mona's performance as a college student. Abigail was also astounded by Mona's enthusiastic approach in relation to the stellar student's extracurricular activities outside of class regarding her two majors at NYU, international affairs and political science. Mona was involved in Student Government. In her undergraduate senior year, she was elected President. Other activities where Mona honed and showcased her skills included Model United Nations, Model Congress, the National Student Leadership Conference, the Association for Public Policy Analysis and Management, and other organizations concerning war, diplomacy, and foreign policy. Mona took courses in international trade in memory of her father, who was an executive in the import/export business. She also took courses in international law in memory of her mother, who was an international affairs attorney at a very prestigious law firm. Abigail was absolutely amazed by Mona Lisa's devotion and the boundless energy that she put into her schoolwork. Mona, through the process, knew how important it was for her to enhance her skills in communication, public speaking, and teamwork. She was also developing into a consummate professional. Mona Lisa Romano was one of, if not the most popular students at NYU. Everyone loved Mona, and she reciprocated that love in an extremely charming manner.

And Abigail and Mona had many, many conversations in the course of Mona Lisa's journey through college. They continued to go out on the town and see all the sights right down to going to shows and musicals at any one of the more than 120 theaters that are off-Broadway. They also ate together at some of the best restaurants in New York City. Abigail and Mona enjoyed each other's company. They had a lot of fun, and people who knew them genuinely had fun being around them.

One night, Abigail was awakened in her condo in the middle of the night by the sound of someone talking. It seemed like it was coming from the living room. Abigail walked down the hallway, and the talking that she had heard distinctly became louder. She could tell that it was Mona talking, but she didn't hear anyone responding to her. When Abigail made it into the living room, Mona was sitting on the couch, still talking out loud, with a textbook in her lap entitled "America's Democracy: The Ideal and the Reality."

"I agree with you. It is possible for the entire world to live in harmony." Mona firmly asserted as she sat on the sofa, looking at the Mona Lisa's portrait on the wall directly in front of her.

"You agree with who that the world can live in harmony, Mona?" Abigail enquired in an assertive manner, wanting to get to the bottom of Mona's behavior.

"My friend," Mona responded, not even seeming startled that Abigail had asked the question after she had entered the living room.

Abigail sat down on the couch next to Mona, most concerned.

"There's no one here but you, Mona. You couldn't be talking to a friend. I could hear you all the way from my bedroom." Abigail's line of questioning was interrupted when she happened to look up at the Mona Lisa's portrait on the wall. "Oh, my goodness! She moved! I distinctly saw the Mona Lisa move in that painting!"

Abigail acted like she had just seen a ghost. And perhaps she had.

"There's nothing to be afraid of, Abigail." Mona calmly reassured.

"She's crazy about you. She knows that you're my friend, and she saw you save my life that night. She knows Daddy wasn't thinking right after losing Mama. And she comforts me by letting me know that Daddy's in a safe place with Mama. Mama forgave Daddy."

"That's who you've been talking to, Mona? The Mona Lisa?" Abigail asked in utter disbelief.

"Yes." Mona politely and serenely stated.

"She's been talking to me for a long time. She's been around for a while, you know. And she's seen a lot of things over the past five centuries or so. And she's shared a lot of those things with me."

"Mona, I can't dispute what you're saying because there is no doubt in my mind that I saw the Mona Lisa move. I have no choice but to believe what you're saying. Oh, there she goes again! I definitely saw her move in that portrait, Mona!" Abigail could not deny Mona's explanation.

"She did it on purpose, Abigail," Mona said in a consoling way.

"She wants you to be aware of what's happening. She loves you. She'd do anything for you. And it would all be for good."

Abigail put her hand over her heart as if she was trying to catch her breath.

"Did your parents know about this, Mona?" Abigail asked.

"I kept the Mona Lisa a secret." Mona gently responded.

"And I can sense that joyful presence again, Mona, just like what we sensed at The Met when we were standing together at the place where her original portrait was once displayed," Abigail exclaimed.

"I know, Abigail. I sense her presence, too, very strongly. I've sensed the Mona Lisa's presence all my life. She desires for good things to take place in our world." Mona Lisa said in a compassionate tone of voice.

Yankee Stadium — New York, New York

New York University Graduation Ceremony

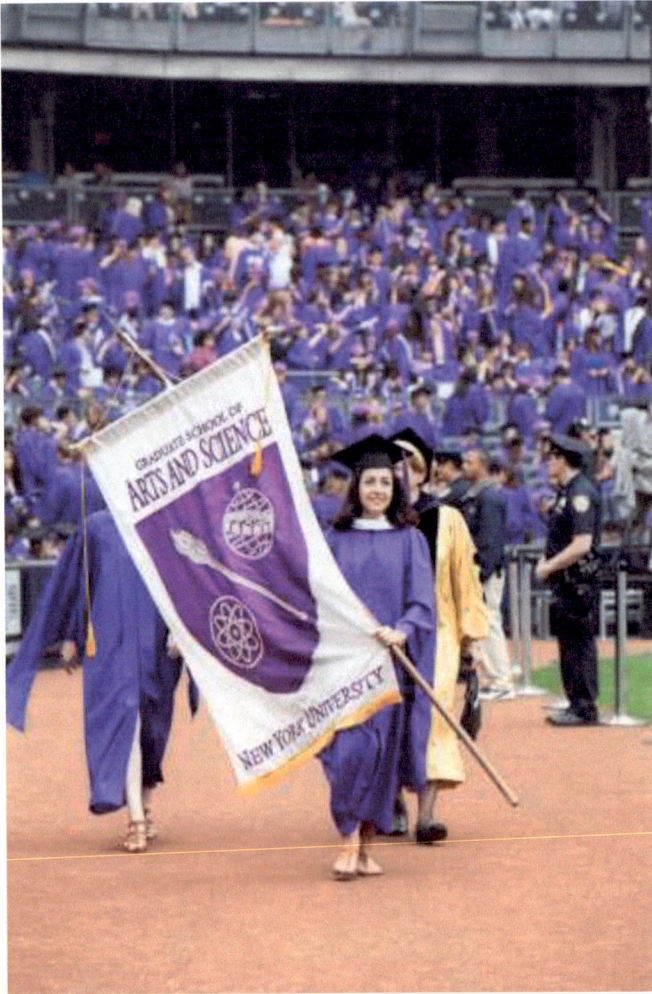

NYU Graduation Pomp And Pageantry

The pomp and pageantry of Mona Lisa Romano's senior class graduation ceremony for NYU was underway. Yankee Stadium, in Bronx, New York (The Bronx), the home of the New York Yankees Major League Baseball Team, was filled to capacity with graduates, family, friends, colleagues, and faculty members, who had eagerly come to celebrate the event. This joyous commencement ceremony was just about to begin.

So many graduates, wearing their purple gowns with black caps bearing a tassel, gathered with high hopes that showed on their faces. The enthusiasm of the entire crowd at the stadium was electrifying. Flags were being flown. NYU banners were being waved. Shouts and screams of elation from well-wishers filled the air. From the podium bearing the New York University purple torch, the Chairman of the Board of Trustees was the first to congratulate all the graduates for beginning their relationship on a life-long basis with their alma mater, New York University. The brand-new NYU graduates were just about to become part of the alumni family. Honorary Degrees were awarded to recipients in various distinguished fields.

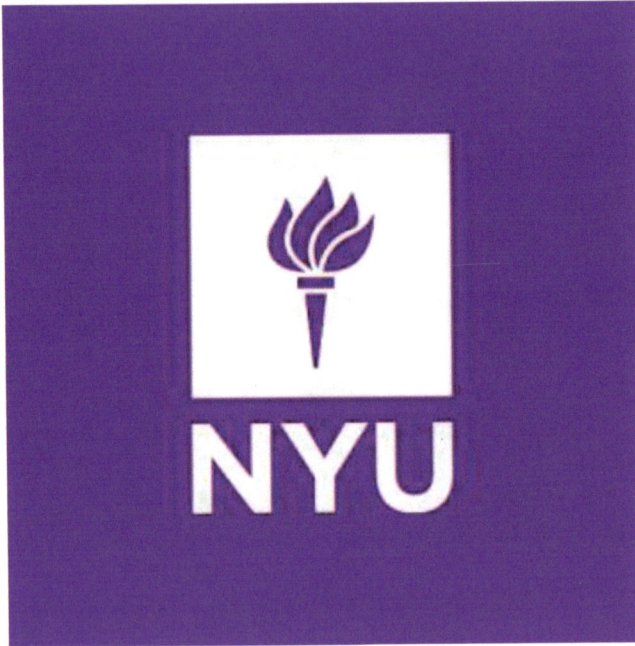

The President of NYU insisted on being the person to introduce Mona Lisa as Valedictorian of this year's senior class.

"Mona Lisa Romano, who many of you know personally, I am very proud to announce, is our Valedictorian for this year's commencement ceremony for our graduating class." The NYU President sincerely shared as the entire audience at Yankee Stadium burst out in applause at the mere mention of Mona's name. The President had to wait a moment for the adulation, clapping, and cheering to die down.

"Mona served as our senior class president this past year with great distinction. She remarkably achieved the Latin academic honor of summa cum laude, earning a perfect 4.0 in both of her majors, international affairs and political science. I know Mona very well, and I am just as impressed with her as a person as I am with her performance. Mona is someone who has touched the lives of many people here at NYU. She has been quite active with the International Relations Society which partners with NYU's Politics Department, bringing students together who are passionate about international affairs, foreign policy, and global events. She has been deeply involved with Model United Nations, learning the art of diplomacy and the principles of how the United Nations functions. She has connected many students with elected officials and progressive organizations through Coalition Z, engaging them in politics to bring about positive change. Her interest in politics and diplomacy has prompted her to participate in prestigious internships that have served to broaden her experience. She has been an active member of the Political Science Club and the Pi Sigma Alpha Political Science

Honor Society. Mona's boundless energy and personable people skills have been most effective in making her one of the single most popular students at New York University. I know some of the challenges that Mona has endured, and I can vouch for the fact that her resilience is absolutely astounding. Ladies and gentlemen, without any further ado, it is a joyful honor for me to present to you NYU's Valedictorian for this year, Mona Lisa Romano."

Everyone, out of love for her, gave Mona Lisa a standing ovation.

"Thank you, Mr. President. Good evening, esteemed faculty of New York University, fellow graduates, proud parents, and distinguished guests. It is from this place today that we will go forth, after much preparation, to make an impact that will change our world for the better." Mona opened enthusiastically, not wasting any time getting her listener's attention. "Our hard work and dedication to our respective fields of endeavor have created the sensation that each and every one of us will make a sizable contribution to producing a hopeful future in a continuously uncertain world that yearns for solid answers to complex questions. All of us present today are representatives of NYU, where science and the arts meet.

We are most aware that life is not measured by the number of breaths we take but by the number of moments that take our breath away. Therefore, at this glorious juncture, we have gathered together in great celebration of this breathtaking moment that we are sharing here and now at Yankee Stadium.

And I am honored to be part of such a special occasion. This could never have been possible without the assistance of so many gifted people. To the exceptional group of administrators, teachers, family, friends, and mentors, especially Dr. Abigail Grant, who all sacrificed above and beyond the call of duty to lead us safely to this point in our journey, I thank you from the bottom of my heart. As I look out at the senior class who I have grown to love so much, what I see are so many fine, young, talented people who are eager to make their own unique mark in the world. This senior class will forever be connected based on the foundation of the many positive memories that we have created together, having shared with each other the passions that we have chosen to pursue. We regard each other as unforgettable people for all time and eternity. As we embark on our extended journey, and my next step will be acquiring a Master's Degree here at NYU, we can take it to heart that success is not necessarily assessed by fame or fortune but by the values that we instill in others, the inspiration we impart that moves others to a place of joy, and the new relationships we continually develop until this entire world is vitally interconnected together in unity.

In our search for meaning, one truth that will become clear to us all is that life is for service. We choose to dedicate our lives to the service of others. We have been given a great deal at NYU to share with the world. And to whom much is given, much is required. And we cannot fail that trust. From here, we move forward. NYU has given us the tools to accel academically, technically, socially, emotionally, and spiritually. During our tenure at NYU, we have been given the opportunity to develop through the arts, sports, and the dedicated instruction of our teachers. We have learned the art of negotiation and the need for comradery. And in this most consequential time of our history, the world needs our gifts.

The world needs our compassion. The world needs our understanding. And the world needs our kindness. These attributes will determine our own destiny and the destinies of those who we touch. There are fundamental questions that our world is posing, and we must be the ones to address these questions. We are the ones who will guarantee a free society. We are the audacious champions who will offer hope. We will fight with all our courage and strength for the dignity of humanity. Our greatest fulfillment will be to make a difference in our world. And when we collectively bring positive change about in our world, it will be worth it. Our endeavor is the liberty of all, with no exception. The responsibility we bear has thrust us into a place of leadership.

And the challenges that we encounter will strengthen our resolve in determining an effective course of action, even in unchartered waters. Through our collective efforts, we will improve our world. And many leaders here at New York University gave us the confidence to believe that we can make a contribution to that improvement.

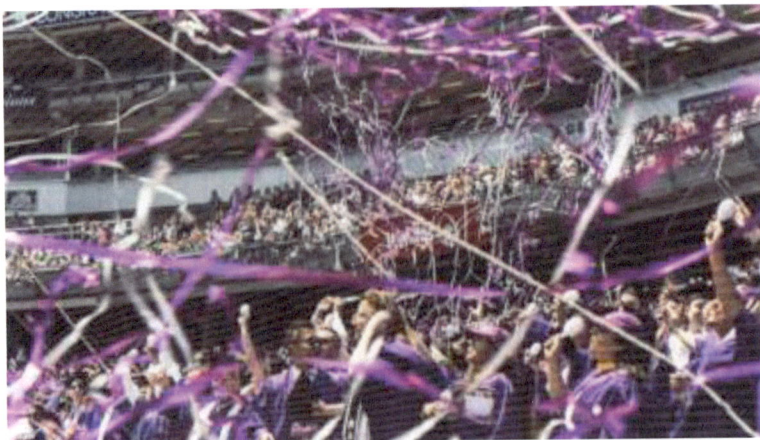

Our motivation to make a positive impact on our world will serve as the impetus that causes us all to achieve new heights each and every day. We're the senior class that will take the steps to do what is right. We are now equipped to make that favorable transformation in our world. And as we set sail upon these new seas, we shall always remember that our home 6wdrport is NYC, with the colors of purple and white. We will always cherish the memories that we have accumulated at New York University. And now, you, my fellow senior class graduates, are the eternal torchbearers for our alma mater, NYU."

The spectators at Yankee Stadium spontaneously stood to their feet in total exhilaration after Mona Lisa Romano's Valedictorian speech.

The applause died down long enough for everyone to hear NYU's President declare: "Mona Lisa, it is most fitting and apropos that you are wearing the color purple as our NYU Valedictorian because, after that stirring speech, you are the very essence of royalty. We are most appreciative of the inspiring words you've just shared in sending our senior class at NYU out into the world. After your presentation, it is safe to say that this graduating class is embarking on its journey with style and substance. We are all very proud of you, Mona. And we will continue to follow your career with high hopes and great expectations. And now, ladies and gentlemen, with that having been said, it is official. You are all now New York University graduates."

Then, all the senior class attending the graduation ceremony burst out again in an echoing reverberation of cheers, throwing their caps high into the air. The excitement was thick.

Considering that the entire faculty was well aware of just how special Abigail was to Mona, Abigail was allowed to sit on the ceremonial stage with the faculty members as the Valedictorian delivered her speech. After Mona Lisa had spoken, Abigail came running up to Mona and threw her arms around the cherished Valedictorian.

"I'm so proud of you, Mona. That was the most beautiful speech I've ever heard." Abigail emotionally declared with tears of joy swelling up in her eyes. Mona Lisa always had Abigail's validation. "You are loved by so many people."

"Thank you. Abigail, I don't know exactly how to explain it, but even more than the thrill of graduating from college and being designated to deliver the Valedictorian speech, I've developed this cognitive ability that I can utilize in so many different ways. And I know that it's something that is going to work for good." Mona exclaimed.

Abigail looked at Mona Lisa with a glow of sheer admiration on her face and said, "Mona, you've learned how to harness your pain!"

As the two embraced in a hug, tears of joy streamed down the cheeks of both Abigail and Mona Lisa for all the progress that had been made.

6

Mona Lisa Romano, as she had stated in her New York University Valedictorian speech, faithfully continued her studies at NYU in international affairs, diplomacy, foreign policy, political science, international law, and international economic trade in relation to the balance of power regarding world order. She also remained very involved with many related extracurricular activities outside the classroom, which solidified her expertise. Before long, Mona Lisa Romano, after a tremendous amount of hard work, earned both her postgraduate Master's Degree and Ph.D. from New York University. Her dissertation, which is a long essay written on a particular subject that is a requirement to obtain a Doctor of Philosophy degree, was entitled "A New Direction." It was a very creative hypothesis of posing how the world could move in a more positive, refreshing direction for the overall benefit of mankind. Mona Lisa's dissertation was hailed by many of her contemporaries and colleagues to be a masterpiece.

In her dissertation, Mona proposed innovative approaches to global diplomacy, emphasizing the importance of cultural empathy and sustainable development. She argued that traditional methods of

98

international relations needed to be revamped to address the complexities of the 21st century, including climate change, cyber threats, and global inequality. Her ideas sparked vigorous debates in academic circles and were published in several prestigious journals, further establishing her as a thought leader in her field.

The White House, Washington, D.C.

During Mona's postgraduate work, she managed to make contacts in Washington, D.C., and she made herself known. Her experience at NYU, along with recommendations from the faculty members at New York University and people she came to know in the world of foreign policy making, caused many people in the U.S. Capital City to regard Mona as a person who meets a very high level of citizenship, professionalism, and loyalty to the United States. Officials in Washington, D.C., felt that Mona could be trusted with America's security and that she could work well in serving the President of the United States. And Mona was also quite capable of rising to the occasion of utilizing her top-notch technical skills.

The National Security Council needed a new Executive Secretary, and Mona Lisa Romano landed the position. The Executive Secretary serves as the chief manager and administrative officer of the National Security Council. Mona would assist in directing the activities of the NSC staff on a broad range of defense, intelligence, and foreign policy matters. All information and actions of the National Security Council staff would be coordinated by Mona, and in turn, she would report all these details to the National Security Advisor and the President. Mona would also serve as the principal point of contact between the National

Security Council and other government agencies, which include the Executive Offices of the President.

In her new role, Mona spearheaded several key initiatives aimed at enhancing inter-agency collaboration. She introduced a secure digital platform for real-time information sharing among various government departments, which significantly improved the efficiency and responsiveness of national security operations. Her innovative approach to problem-solving and her ability to think strategically under pressure were highly praised by her colleagues and superiors.

The National Security Council office is located in the West Wing of the White House, not far from the Oval Office of the President. Mona Lisa Romano loved working with the National Security Council, and she performed her duties with joy. It gave Mona the opportunity to hone her ability to coordinate national security and foreign policies among various government agencies and a perfect venue to showcase her negotiating and diplomatic prowess. The people she worked with at the White House found her to be most qualified for the position of Executive Secretary. They also regarded Mona to be an extremely charming person.

Mona's charm was not merely superficial; it was rooted in her deep empathy and understanding of human nature. She made a point to learn about the personal backgrounds and motivations of her colleagues, which helped her build strong, trusting relationships within the NSC. Her leadership style was inclusive and empowering, encouraging team members to contribute their best ideas and collaborate effectively.

One of Mona's most significant contributions during her tenure was the development of a comprehensive strategy to counter emerging cyber threats. Recognizing the growing importance of cybersecurity in national defense, she coordinated with leading experts from the private sector, academia, and international allies to create a robust framework for protecting America's digital infrastructure. This strategy not only strengthened national security but also positioned the United States as a global leader in cybersecurity innovation.

Through her work, Mona gained the respect and admiration of influential figures in Washington, D.C., and beyond. She was frequently invited to speak at international conferences and think tanks, where she shared her insights on global security and diplomacy. Her eloquence and expertise made her a sought-after advisor on critical issues facing the international community.

7

The Capitol Building, Washington, D.C.

When the current United States President was sworn into office for his first term at the United States Capitol building by Chief Justice of the Supreme Court, Archibald William Hand, he stated the words from Article I, Section 3 of the United States Constitution, with his right hand raised and his left hand on the Bible:

"I, Alexander Hampton White, do solemnly swear that I will faithfully execute the Office of President of the United States, and will to the best of my ability preserve, protect, and defend the Constitution of the United States." And what that means is that the President will work to guarantee every American their fundamental human rights in a free democracy and protection of everyone's life, liberty, and property.

The President of the United States is, obviously, an extremely busy person. That fact is no less true for the current President, Alexander Hampton White. An incoming president makes 4,000 political appointments upon taking office, 1,200 of which must be confirmed by the Senate. In many other countries, the head of state is a monarch or a president, and then separately, there is also a head of government, such as a prime minister or premier.

On the other hand, in the United States, the two positions are combined into one, hence, the President of the United States. The President is both the head of the government, with actual political powers and responsibilities, and the head of state, with ceremonial and symbolic duties as well. In the United States of America, the President is the Commander in Chief of State, the national leader ultimately overseeing the safety and security of the United States and its citizens, who exercise supreme command and control over the military branches of the armed forces. He is the designated government official who is over the Executive Branch, emotionally identified with many people in America and all around the world. Many people who vicariously relate to his strong leadership have very high expectations of the President of the United States and put him on a pedestal equivalent to that of a superstar. People look to the President to be tough enough to stand up to a threatening foreign adversary yet understanding enough to fight for the rights and concerns of the American people, as well as other countries. The vitality of democracy rests on the shoulders of the President of the United States in regard to each and every decision and action he takes. There have been times in American history when the President stretched the limits of the United States Constitution.

And especially since the end of World War II, when nuclear weapons and weapons of mass destruction came to prominence, the policy questions that the federal government has had to answer became more complex. The

United States Congress increasingly left more and more details of new policies and programs up to the various executive departments and agencies over which the President presides. The expanded federal role in international and domestic affairs concerning military and economic matters, therefore, has extended the power of the Presidency. And the President has gained enormous power as a result of America's emergence as a world power in the nuclear age. The President has become the leader of the free world. The President's finger is on the nuclear red button. And national security and national defense require that the President act quickly in the event of an emergency. Yet, despite how much information the President may have at his disposal, there is still no guarantee the world will not find itself engulfed in the flames of nuclear holocaust and destruction. Media attention has encouraged the people of the world to feel that the President of the United States must intervene in all problems and policies of the nuclear age, expecting him to have all the answers. The President is, by the Constitution, the Chief Executive and head of the Executive Branch of the government. The President must deal with Congress. He has great influence over the House of Representatives and the Senate. The President is an important participant on the world stage of international affairs and foreign policy, especially with respect to issues of war and peace. All the hats that the President of the United States wears are grounded in the Constitution. As Chief Executive, the President presides over the Executive Office, which includes the White House staff, as well as the Cabinet Departments, independent agencies, regulatory boards, and commissions. In addition to the White House staff, the Executive Office of the President is made up of several relatively special, permanent offices, which are headed by presidential appointees. The President nominates United States Supreme Court judges, with the appointments subject to approval from the Senate.

The President has the power to negotiate matters of diplomacy and sign treaties with foreign countries. These treaties go into effect after being ratified by a two-thirds vote in the Senate. In regard to foreign policymaking, the implementation of these policies, and diplomacy, the President appoints the United States Secretary of State, U.S. Ambassadors to foreign countries as well as to the United Nations, and the National Security Advisor. And right now, President Alexander White was in dire straits to fill one of his key positions.

"Breaking news here in Washington. There are reports from the White House that President White's National

Security Advisor, Gary Dixon, is skating on thin ice. His expected departure doesn't appear to be a matter of if but when. This comes less than a year after President Alexander White began his first term in office. The President has yet to comment on Mr. Dixon's status. The details, at this point, are being kept under wraps. The only information we're receiving is that the cover-up may have been even worse than the crime itself. But what we do know for a certainty is that the National Security Advisor has ruffled the feathers of a number of White House Administration officials, and that includes the President. Mr. Dixon may very well be working at the White House now on borrowed time. The National Security Advisor is not a member of the Cabinet. Therefore, the President can pick a new National Security Advisor on his own, without a vote from the Senate being necessary. Benjamin Brown, CBS News, the White House."

Gary Dixon, the current National Security Advisor, had caused an embarrassing scandal and needed to be replaced. The situation had become so complex that even President White was all for the idea of seeking a replacement.

Soon afterward, the President's desk was swamped with many file folders of eligible candidates for the coveted job of National Security Advisor. While the National Security Council is chaired by the President of the United States, its regular attendees include the Vice President of the United States, the U.S. Secretary of State, the U.S. Secretary of Treasury, the U.S. Secretary of Defense, and the Assistant to the President for National Security Affairs. The National Security Advisor reports directly to the President. The National Security Advisor also works with the Homeland Security Council. The National Security Council's Executive Office is based in the West Wing of the White House, where the President's Oval Office is located. While the United States Secretary of State is the President's chief foreign affairs advisor, carrying out the President's foreign policies through the State Department and the Foreign Service of the United States, the National Security Advisor offers the President a wide range of options on national security issues. The National Security Advisor's other duties include assistance in planning the President's foreign travel and providing background memos and staffing for the President's meetings, summits, and phone calls with world leaders. The National Security Advisor and the Secretary of State confer with each other on a regular basis.

In regard to other White House concerns, United States President Alexander White and his wife were extremely popular in France, and it gave the First Lady an interesting idea. Her great appreciation of the arts prompted her to request that the French Republic allow her to exhibit the original Mona Lisa portrait in Washington, D.C. The current First Lady's French ancestry and the recent visit to France with the President didn't hurt matters. But rather than having the painting displayed at the National Gallery of Art in Washington, D.C., as Jacqueline Bouvier Kennedy made it possible in 1963, she would have it exhibited in the East Room of the White House for tourists to admire.

The White House Exhibiting The Mona Lisa In The East Room

The President of France, Regis Delon, granted the First Lady's request. Once the famous portrait was displayed in a bulletproof case in the East Room, the First Lady anxiously took the President by the hand and led him to the Mona Lisa for a private viewing. As the President and the First Lady stood before the Mona Lisa, admiring her beauty, an overwhelming feeling completely overpowered the Chief

Executive. The President's reaction to Leonardo da Vinci's most well-known work of art was quite apparent to the First Lady.

"Are you all right, Dear?" The First Lady uneasily asked.

"I think so." The President said.

"I can't explain it exactly, but looking at that portrait is having some kind of effect on me." The President said, having no idea what was occurring.

"The Mona Lisa has a way about her that intrigues people." The First Lady rationalized.

"No. It's something much more formidable than that, Emily." The President insisted.

"As I had mentioned, I simply can't explain what's happening. Whatever it may be is too intense to ignore, and I can't tell if it's going to stop or not, even after we leave the East Room. I can't make any sense of this!"

The President eventually made his way back to the Oval Office. He stood behind his desk, still reeling from his recent encounter with the Mona Lisa portrait. He looked down at the top of his desk and noticed his list of candidates for National Security Advisor. One name on the list that he hadn't noticed before leaped off the page and grabbed his attention: Dr. Mona Lisa Romano. The President found her file and studied it with amazement. Alexander Hampton White knew who Mona Ramona was, of course, but not in depth.

"I must interview this young lady." The President said out loud to himself.

And before long, it happened. Dr. Mona Lisa Romano, candidate for National Security Advisor for the United States of America, was seated in the Oval Office directly across from the President. Mona sat there very poised, radiating her usual sweet disposition.

President Alexander White With Mona Romano

"Dr. Romano, I'd sincerely like to thank you for meeting with me today." President White said to open the conversation.

"It is a tremendous honor for me, Mr. President!" Mona exclaimed, yet remaining totally composed.

"If you knew the process that it took to get you here today, which I personally witnessed, Dr. Romano, you'd fully realize that I'm the one who is genuinely honored." President White stated from his heart.

"I've had a chance to review your file, and while you are younger and somewhat less experienced than the other candidates, your record is impeccable!"

"Thank you, Mr. President," Mona said.

"My life is all about diplomacy, negotiating, policymaking, and implementing foreign policy."

"First of all, I would like to mention that I had a chance to read the dissertation that you wrote entitled 'A New Direction' when you were in pursuit of your Ph.D. at New York University. And I must say, Dr. Romano, I have never read anything so eloquent in my life. It was most original, substantial, and pertinent. And I never imagined that a contribution in the field of international affairs could be so charming! Your dissertation entitled 'A New Direction' is refreshingly innovative."

"Thank you, President White," Mona responded with great enthusiasm.

"A number of United States Presidents, with great fierceness, strong conviction, and determination, have embraced the preservation, enhancement, and expansion of human rights, urging the American people and other countries to completely accept democracy in its purest form. I have known you to be this kind of President for some time now, urging the defense and values of democracy and ushering in important changes regarding the human condition for our world. I know you are an advocate of the modernization of the Peace of Westphalia, which is the collective name for two treaties that were signed in October of 1648, putting an end to the Thirty Years War. It was the single most deadly European war of religion. The Peace of Westphalia ceased a horrible period of calamity in European history. The Thirty Year's War had resulted in an estimated eight million deaths. The Peace of Westphalia ultimately brought peace to the Holy Roman Empire after an extremely long and complex negotiation process. The Peace of Westphalia is identified as the origin and foundation of principles that are crucial to modern international relations. One big reason the Thirty Years War ended is because the recognition to bring peace about became abundantly clear and imperative. I feel that's a reality that our entire world is facing today, especially in direct regard to putting an end to long periods of religious conflicts that have hindered, prevented, and misinterpreted the understanding of the concept of democracy for centuries. It appears that the abuse of religion in the pursuit of power is a reality that has unfortunately been echoing throughout the corridors of time. It is a dilemma that has been handed down to our modern age, contributing to a horrific imbalance in power among the nations of the world. The United States needs the kind of strategy and diplomacy that will comprehend, accommodate, and effectively confront the complexity of our upcoming journey. Many factors have caused a misinterpretation of the significance, need, and productive power of democracy. Of course, the aspiration for a unified, progressive, and positive global system must be completely multilateral. The question that we must consider here is whether our negotiating, policymaking, and diplomatic efforts will always be ongoing to the end of time, requiring adjustments as we move forward, or are these efforts actually serving to bring the nations of Earth to a place that ultimately concludes with permanent, international peace in our world, that is, a peace we all may cherish and revel in."

President White just sat there for several seconds in his Oval Office chair with an inquisitive smile on his face after listening to Mona. He was very impressed, even tickled, by what Mona had just graphically expressed. But at the same time, his intrigue was mixed with the challenge of attempting to understand exactly what made this delightful, capable young lady tick. Nevertheless, President White continued his interview.

"You're right on target, Dr. Romano. I am an advocate of the modernization of the Peace of Westphalia principles. The implementation and employment of these policies patterned on today's trajectory could make all the difference in our international relations. Effective policymaking with these truths and propositions as our foundation could very well accelerate world peace. Just as these principles managed to end a great deal of potential human carnage that would have continued to take place in the Thirty Years War, it also laid the framework for a system of competing, independent European states. These principles presumed that each country has sovereignty over its own territory and domestic affairs without interference from another country and yet, at the same time, is equal in international law. Now, of course, a lot of big decisions are made by my National Security Advisor in the course of each day. What is your personal interpretation of taking on the position of National Security Advisor?" The President enquired.

"Yes. Since its inception under President Harry Truman, the National Security Advisor has spearheaded the National Security Council, whose chief function is to advise and assist the President on national security and foreign policies," Mona indicated.

"The Council also serves as the President's principal arm for coordinating these policies among various U.S. government agencies. While the National Security Advisor is not a Cabinet level position like the United States Secretary of State, he or she does make many critical decisions. The National Security Advisor is the President's right-hand person because he or she serves as the principal advisor to the President on all national security issues. To be effective as a National Security Advisor, one would need to be fast on his or her feet as a critical thinker, have stellar communication skills, and be able to handle high pressure situations with a certain degree of grace and finesse. Being a National Security Advisor requires you to be a top-notch problem solver. The National Security Advisor is the personal advisor to the President, usually advising him every day. He or she is over the meetings where various agencies get together at the direction of the President to make every effort to solve certain priority issues. The National Security Advisor oversees the development, implementation, and execution of foreign policies on behalf of the United States, speaking publicly to promote the President's foreign policies. He or she is also involved in the negotiating process. All aspects of any problem that the White House confronts should be exposed. A certain degree of transparency is expected by the American people and the media. Of course, this information is coordinated in an organized manner and should be tailored for the President to assist him in his decision-making process. Many times, it's a matter of administrative advisors presenting every side of a situation through many various strong views and disagreements in complete candor in the face of a crisis and then allowing the President to make a decision. At that point, everyone is clear on what exactly is the way forward. A National Security Advisor must be straightforward concerning what the intelligence suggests about what the United States should do. The National Security Advisor must provide the President with a range of choices to choose from. The heart of the position is monitoring the pulse of the National Security Council, which brings together the State Department, the Pentagon, the Intelligence Agencies, military advisors of the armed forces, and all strategy-making departments engaging in foreign policy to formulate effective policy and have it implemented. The National Security Council assists the President in figuring out and determining what policy options should be considered, and then oversees the process of how they will be implemented, that is, talking through the most difficult operational issues."

Mona Lisa Romano was everything and more that the President expected her to be. He found Mona's natural charm to be most refreshing. Mona was meek but, at the same time, very forthright. Her formidable fortitude was evident. The President was dazzled by Mona's expertise and aptitude in international affairs. She knew exactly what she was talking about.

"Dr. Romano, tell me how you feel about China's threat to Taiwan these days." The President asked.

"China continues to show hostile aggression toward Taiwan. Taiwan is a country that has not had a seat in the United Nations for over half a century. It's a very precarious situation. We continue to see signs of Chinese escalation, including new forces positioning an invasion fleet to overwhelm the Taiwanese shoreline. An invasion could begin at any time. The United States needs to, now more than ever, demonstrate how to escalate result-oriented diplomacy focused on the security of Taiwan. The United States also needs to be ready to respond decisively, alongside all those allies who support Taiwan, should China choose to take military action. American forces should be ready to strategically support Taiwan. NATO may have no ambitions to become a military alliance in the Indo-Pacific region, but NATO should strongly discourage China from taking any actions that will alter the status quo of Taiwan. Further economic sanctions against China should be considered if they take further military action, with similar actions taken by other partners of Taiwan. The situation has already led to a significant international response, including various sanctions targeting Chinese industries, financial transactions, and trade routes aimed at curbing their aggressive policies.

This situation is extremely serious. But it should be mentioned that Russia does not feel strongly enough about Taiwan to get involved." Mona responded in a nutshell.

"Mona," the President responded, addressing Dr. Romano by her first name for the first time, obviously approving of her answer, "What is your personal take on the crisis in the Middle East?"

"The Middle East, President White, is a region that is a world of disorder unto itself. Nowhere is the challenge of international order more complex than the obstacles that are present in the Middle East. It all goes as far back as the third millennium B.C. when Egypt expanded its influence along the Nile River and into present-day Sudan. In the exact same period, the empires of Mesopotamia, Sumer, and Babylon consolidated their rule over people along the Tigris and Euphrates rivers. In the sixth century B.C., the Persian Empire emerged on the Iranian plateau and developed a system of governing principles that is considered to be an intentional attempt to unite the African, Asian, and European countries into one single organized international society. By the end of the sixth century A.D., two empires controlled the Middle East: The Byzantine or Eastern Roman Empire, with its capital in Constantinople advocating Christianity, and the Sassanid Persian Empire, with its capital near modern-day Baghdad practicing Zoroastrianism, one of the world's oldest religions. The two empires became involved in a twenty-five-year-long war that led to a Byzantine victory. And what statesmanship failed to do, total exhaustion that resulted from the war managed to produce peace. But this opened up the door for the Prophet Muhammad and his followers from western Arabia to fulfill his vision of replacing all the prevailing religious faiths in the region, especially Judaism, Christianity, and Zoroastrianism, with Islam. Islam's rapid advance across three continents convinced many loyalists of their divine mission to enforce a new world order. After the Prophet Muhammad's death, Islam split into the two branches of Sunni Islam and Shiite Islam, which is a defining division in the contemporary Islamic world. Eventually, the Ottoman Empire, otherwise known as the Turkish Empire, emerged as one of the mightiest and longest-lasting Islamic-run superpowers in the world in 1299. This empire officially collapsed in 1922, resulting in Turkey being declared a republic. The Ottomans also interpreted their mission as upholding the order of the world, but this plan failed when the Ottoman Empire chose to side with Germany during World War I. After World War I, the League of Nations, which the United States never joined, divided the Ottoman Empire. And up to World War II, the European powers were sufficiently strong in maintaining the regional order that they had designed in the Middle East. Another significant factor is the British government's 1917 Balfour Declaration announcing an initiative to establish Israel as the homeland of the Jewish people. During World War II, 5.5 million Muslims participated on the Allied side of the war.

The Second World War had a momentous impact on the Islamic world. With the advance of Japanese troops into Southeast Asia and Italian and German military involvement in North Africa, Muslim-populated lands became front-line zones. As a result, nearly 1.5 million Muslims were killed during World War II. Six million Jews were killed in the Holocaust. Around 419,000 Americans, 24,000,000 Soviets, and 451,000 British people, military and civilian, died in World War II. An estimated total of 75 to 85 million people perished in World War II, and at least 40 million of these people were civilians, making it the deadliest conflict in human history. Cold War-era relations between the Islamic and the non-Islamic nations complied with a balance-of-power-based approach. Egypt, Syria, Algeria, and Iraq generally supported Soviet policies, while Israel, Jordan, Saudi Arabia, and Morocco were friendly with the United States, relying on U.S. support for their security. Israel became a State in 1948, and intense conflicts between the Israelis and neighboring Muslim countries have taken place ever since, in 1948, 1956, 1967, and 1973, for a start. Before long, in 1988, al-Qaeda, a global terrorist movement, was founded. Hamas, the Afghan Taliban, Hezbollah, ISIS, and many other jihadist groups were also formed.

Of course, the attitudes of radical Muslims do not reflect the peaceful inclination of many other Muslims, but radical Islam today is one of the biggest factors to consider in regard to pursuing a healthy balance of power among the nations of our modern world. And, of course, another factor tipping the balance of power seesaw in the Middle East is Iran's nuclear capability. The issue of peace in the Middle East is centered around the delicate topic of Iran's possession of nuclear weapons. And in view of this factor, the risk of an Israeli preemptive attack rises significantly. Also, there are countless complications caused by the Sunni-Shia civil wars taking place in many Arab states. The Palestinian issue will have to be resolved as an essential element of regional, if not international, order. Mr. President, I believe a new dimension of fortitude and vision is required in the Middle East. Out of all the regions in the world, more wars spring up in the Middle East than anywhere else."

Once again, the President just sat there, taking in a thoughtful moment, trying to figure out how a harmless, innocent-looking, fragile, young lady like Mona could possibly be so meticulously well-versed on such harsh, complex matters as the history of foreign relations, international affairs, and nuclear weapons policy implications. The President was astonished by Mona's cognition. But of course, President White was more than composed enough to press on with his interview.

"Just one final question, Mona." The President said intently.

"We've discussed the necessity for cohesive world order. One major dilemma in regard to world order concerns us with a single question: Can the many various, diverse countries' views of world order be reconciled, especially in relation to Asia?"

"Mr. President," Mona immediately responded, "The conditions for Westphalian diplomacy only began to be utilized with the decolonization that took place following the devastation of European order, which was caused by the two world wars of the twentieth century. Also, after World War II, Asia witnessed the Korean War, the Sino-Soviet confrontation from 1955-1980, the Vietnam War, the four India-Pakistan wars, the Chinese-India War, the Chinese-Vietnam War, and a number of other conflicts. The process of producing emancipation and regional order in Asia has been quite violent. Yet, after decades of war and turmoil, Asia has drastically transformed itself. The rise of the Asian Tigers has brought prosperity and vigorous economic activity to Hong Kong, South Korea, Singapore, Taiwan, and Thailand. Japan is a free democracy, enjoying freedom, peace, and prosperity through economic diplomacy. Article 9 of the Constitution of Japan outlaws war as a means to settle international disputes and relies on American military strength to compensate. Even China has changed course to the extent that there has been a transformative effect on their relations with the rest of the world. And as these changes have unfolded, foreign policy, premised on Westphalian principles, has prevailed in Asia. Various nations in Asia, making a departure from the colonial period, are committed to noninterference in one another's national domestic affairs. And while United States diplomacy efforts of embracing democracy need to be maintained, Asia has emerged as a very strong advocate of the Westphalian system. However, India is not interested in being a member of an international system. India is focused on their own security, on a regional level only. In addition to its enhanced economic influence and military power, India has significantly increased its stockpile of nuclear weapons. And India has surpassed China as Asia's most populated nation. India's role in world order is complicated by its complex relationships with countries like China, Afghanistan, Pakistan, and Bangladesh. Ever since the end of World War II, border disputes between these nations have caused military clashes, terrorist infiltration, and senseless violence. Pakistan also is heavily vested with weapons of mass destruction. Of course, China has had nuclear weapons since 1964. Afghanistan may not have nuclear weapons, but they have a strong relationship with India, which has avoided alienating the Taliban. India pursues a policy of close collaboration with Afghanistan. Russia supplies military support to the Taliban. And China is committed to a foreign policy of friendship in Afghanistan, especially on an economic basis. And while the transformation in China may be considered to be progressive, the Chinese people are not interested in being converted to democracy, as it is defined in the United States. The People's Republic of China is a one-party state ruled by the Chinese Communist Party, which is based on democratic centralism, a combination of classic Marxism and Leninism organizational ideology. Bangladesh has been receiving ongoing shipments of uranium fuel in collaboration with the Russian atomic company, Rosatom, to produce nuclear energy. And while Muslims may make up a minority group in China, it still accounts for 20 million people. Afghanistan is practically 100% Muslim, with 90% following Sunni Islam and 10% following Shiite Islam. Almost all the people in Pakistan are Muslim. There are 172 million Muslims in India, with 94% of the population being Hindu at over a billion people. 80% of the people in Bangladesh are Muslim. So, while the Muslims of these various nations in Asia have conflicts with each other, Russia is allied with each and every one of them, including China. And, of course, that is a factor that severely complicates matters for the United States. President White, no truly lasting, positive world order has ever existed. The founding fathers of the United States laid the foundations of a distinct vision of world order for the New World. They demanded independence in the name of Westphalian concepts. America's vision of the Westphalian system has not been based on the European pattern of balance of power but on the achievement of peace through the dynamic of democracy. It is upon this premise that modern Westphalian concepts will be recognized as the sole basis for an existing, realistic world order that will be unshakable. In our modern world, a newly revised, up-to-date, contemporary Westphalian system based on democracy needs to reach out and extend to all nations to create a congenial global world order, or, I should say, colloquially, in the conversational vernacular, a harmonious world community. And international peace will serve to bring about a balance of power that will enhance the welfare of every nation on Earth. This will be a pluralistic international order that advocates a system in which all the nations of the world, with the many various array of people, beliefs, opinions, outlooks, and needs, will coexist in utter peace. I am convinced that only democracy, in its purest form, can make this a reality. The history of prior civilizations is a redundant tale of the rise and fall of empires. But a world that embraces the peace that is derived from solid, contemporary Westphalian principles of democracy will never subside."

"Thank you, Mona." The President said, with a tone of favor in his voice.

"You have been most articulate in explaining an extremely complex situation in understandable terms. And in my opinion, three-fourths of the battle in diplomacy is speaking clearly enough so that everyone is on the same page. Now, while you have extensive experience working as the National Security Council's Executive Secretary, that is, serving as chief manager and administrative manager of the National Security Council, during this period, you have played a significant role in developing and implementing effective United States foreign policy in many critical parts of the world. You've directed the activities of the National Security Council staff on a broad range of defense, intelligence, and foreign policy matters. You have effectively coordinated information and actions regarding matters of diplomacy that the NSC staff has submitted to you and properly forwarded these vital details in an understandable manner to the National Security Advisor and myself. You have been on the advisory board that advocates progressive American leadership, and you have attended and taught courses related to your expertise at one of America's top universities, NYU. You have also been involved with many impressive extracurricular activities academically in regard to international affairs and foreign policy all the way up to the point when you acquired your Ph.D. from New York University. After speaking with you today, it is most apparent to me that you are well aware that the work of diplomacy is not successful solely through a vast acquisition of knowledge, but also by having the ability to make correct snap decisions. Mona, I haven't gone out on a limb for any of the other National Security Advisor candidates, but I'm going to make an exception in your case by letting you know that you are definitely in the running for the position. As you know, we have the World Summit coming up next month, and I'm going to need my National Security Advisor with me. I do plan on making my decision promptly, and no matter what direction is taken, I would like to personally take this opportunity to thank you for making such a substantial contribution to the National Security Council, serving in the capacity of Executive

Secretary. Please do not leave the Oval Office today without fully realizing that you are greatly appreciated, and it has been a pleasure getting to know you up close and personal."

Both Mona and President White stood up together. The President firmly shook Mona's extended hand.

"Thank you, President White," Mona said modestly, with a smile that came very close to making the President gasp. President White's mind flashed naturally to the portrait of the Mona Lisa created by Leonardo da Vinci, that just so happened to be located in the East Room of the White House.

"Having a pioneering United States President like yourself, taking on the challenges of our momentous age, is meant to be."

President Alexander White kept standing as Mona Lisa Romano gracefully exited the Oval Office. Afterward, he just sat in his chair for the longest time, figuratively scratching his head.

8

The White House

"Molly, contact Dr. Abigail Grant in Manhattan and see if she'll agree to me having her flown into Washington. Let Dr. Grant know that I would like to meet with her. You'll find her contact information in Mona Romano's file." The President requested.

"Right away, President White." Molly, the President's secretary and personal aide, responded.

It didn't take Abigail long to figure out why the President wanted to see her. Even a United States President was intrigued enough by Mona to try to get a few questions answered about her. Mona had that effect on many people.

Abigail shook the President's hand prior to getting comfortable in a White House Oval Office chair in front of Alexander Hampton White's desk.

President Alexander White with Dr. Abigail Grant

"Thank you very much for taking the time to meet with me, Dr. Grant." The President said politely.

"It's most gracious of you."

"I consider it to be an honor to meet you in person, Mr. President," Abigail said.

"I'm certain you've surmised why I've asked you to meet with me." The President deducted.

"Yes. It would be a rhetorical question to ask you why I'm here. It obviously concerns Mona Lisa. You're possibly attempting to, shall we say, figure her out." Abigail safely presumed, carefully selecting her words.

"That's an excellent way of putting it, Dr. Grant." The President responded, acting somewhat relieved that he may be acquiring some explanation from an authority and a reliable source about Mona.

"She's quite a young lady. I can see that you've gathered that much about her, Mr. President." Abigail keenly noticed.

"Yes. Mona is, indeed, an extremely impressive young lady. As you know, she is one of the candidates that I am seriously considering to be my National Security Advisor, despite the fact that she's only twenty-five years old."

"Has something in particular taken place, Mr. President, to pique your curiosity about Mona?" Abigail suspected.

"Yes, Dr. Grant. Something quite out of the ordinary has occurred." The President said with a puzzled look on his face.

"I am most appreciative that a person of your caliber and credibility has chosen to meet with me and hopefully offer some insight. Mona is a very charming person. I believe she's qualified for the position of National Security Advisor. But there is a disarming element of mystery about her, and I need to get some questions answered." The President said candidly.

"Mr. President, let me ask you: Does your concern about Mona Romano have anything to do with the fact that the Mona Lisa portrait is on display at the White House right now?" Abigail asked about it as gently as she possibly could.

"That, Dr. Grant, is the one-million-dollar question right there!" The President said, fully realizing, at this very point, that Abigail was aware of a link between Mona Lisa Romano and the Mona Lisa portrait.

"It's funny. I'm amazed that you just asked me that question, but at the same time, I'm not one bit surprised."

"I can perfectly understand how you feel," Abigail said in an understanding manner.

"What can you tell me about this situation, Dr. Grant? I'd appreciate any and all clarification that you can provide." The President was quite earnest.

"Mr. President, you are correct in assessing that there is a connection between Mona and the Mona Lisa."

"Well, Dr. Grant, I honestly feel that I could not be getting that fact confirmed by a better source than yourself. My wife and I were standing in front of the Mona Lisa one evening, and something very odd and unexplainable took place. Shortly after encountering a profound sensation upon viewing the Mona Lisa, I came back to the Oval Office, looked down at my desk at my candidate list for National Security Advisor, and Mona Lisa Romano's name leaped up at me off the page. It was the very first time that I had noticed her as a candidate on the list. Very shortly afterward, I interviewed Mona here in the Oval Office where you're sitting right now, and if I didn't know better, I would say that the Mona Lisa was attempting, in spirit, to persuade me to appoint Mona Lisa Romano then and there, right on the spot. I must admit that it took some sheer willpower on my part to not give in to that inclination. Even now, I can sense that the Mona Lisa is disappointed that I did not comply, despite it having been an impulsive move without a little more consideration of the other candidates."

"Mr. President, it's not your imagination. The Mona Lisa really is attempting to persuade you to get Mona Romano on board as your National Security Advisor. It's what she wants. It's not a coincidence that her portrait is in the White House at the very same time when you interviewed Mona for National Security Advisor. The Mona Lisa has probably seen your meeting with Mona coming for many, many years!"

"But how can that be possible? And if it's true, exactly what is the Mona Lisa attempting to accomplish by influencing me to have Mona as my National Security Advisor? Do you feel that there is anything subversive taking place here?" The President asked, as long as they were on the topic of national security.

"No. I honestly do not think that subversion is an issue here. The Mona Lisa's intention is certainly not to undermine an established system of government. I believe it's quite the opposite. I think that the desired outcome is to be something of a very positive and constructive nature." Abigail reassured.

"And you feel that you're familiar enough with this situation to be qualified to make a statement like that with assurance, Dr. Grant?" The President enquired.

"Yes, Mr. President. And not just based on what I've seen and heard. Because my personal experience of all this has caused me to do a considerable amount of research of my own on the matter." Abigail revealed.

"What kind of research?" The President asked.

Leonardo Da Vinci, The Genius

"Well, in order to better understand the Mona Lisa, it's necessary to understand her creator, Leonardo da Vinci." Abigail pointed out.

"He's the genius behind the masterpiece. He was born in the heart of the Renaissance in the spring of 1452 on April

15th. The Renaissance was a period of great cultural rebirth and awakening, and Leonardo personified that spirit of renewal, exploration, and innovation. He was born in Vinci, Italy, a commune of the metropolitan city of Florence in the Italian region of Tuscany. His curiosity was sparked at a young age. The rolling hills, winding rivers, and diversity of nature served as inspiration for his artistic and scientific pursuits. His unconventional education and unique experiences shaped his view of the world, an outlook that blended the lines between art and science, observation and invention. He moved to Florence as a teenager, where he apprenticed under the renowned artist, Andrea del Verrocchio. This was a pivotal time in Leonardo's life as he honed his skills in drawing, painting, and sculpting. He also began to develop his scientific understanding. His insatiable curiosity led him to explore a wide range of subjects, including engineering, architecture, biology, astronomy, botany, art, robotics, theater design, and aviation. He was a scientist, an artist, and an inventor."

"Yes. Leonardo da Vinci is one of the few people who is a jack of all trades and a master of all trades as well." The President commented.

"I've always been fascinated by him."

"And rightly so. Leonardo, Mr. President, was not just one of the greatest geniuses who ever lived. He was the greatest genius who ever lived." Abigail was compelled to make the distinction.

"His meticulous detail and relentless pursuit of excellence are evident in each of his works. With her enigmatic smile and serene gaze, the Mona Lisa is the ultimate testament to Leonardo da Vinci's genius and a supreme symbol of his ability to merge art and science, emotion and intellect. When Leonardo embarked on his project of painting the Mona Lisa in 1503, I believe he even realized that he would be immortalizing his name in the annals of art history. The creation of the Mona Lisa was a labor of love. Leonardo may not have even realized it initially when he began painting the Mona Lisa, but in the process, somewhere along the line, he began to realize he was creating a masterpiece, background and all, that could literally alter the destiny of mankind!"

"It does appear that he painted the Mona Lisa with a very intent purpose." The President noted.

"And I can definitely determine that you have done some perceptive reading between the lines of Leonardo da Vinci. Please go on."

"There's no question about it, Mr. President." Abigail continued.

"I have developed a great deal of insight into Leonardo's life that goes way beyond history books. I've had to, for Mona's sake. And the expertise that he engaged when he painted the Mona Lisa played a crucial role in emphasizing, exemplifying, and enhancing that purpose. One unique technique he used was sfumato, which is Italian for the word, 'smoky.' He employed many brown and yellow shades. It involves the delicate layering of translucent glazes, creating soft transitions between colors and tones. It's what gives the Mona Lisa her almost ethereal, dream-like quality. Leonardo masterfully applied his brushstrokes to distinguish the lines between reality and illusion. He was a keen observer of the natural world, and that's definitely reflected in the Mona Lisa. Her pose reveals a complex understanding of light and darkness, three-dimensional depth, and human form that makes the Mona Lisa appear tangible. Another technique he used was employing geometry in the painting. The detailed landscape background of the portrait is a major part of the story that Leonardo wants to tell through the Mona Lisa. The winding paths, the water, the distant mountains, and the bridge are not just a backdrop but an integral part of the overall composition, adding depth and mystery to the painting that cries out for explanation. Yet, there are no clear boundaries between the background and the Mona Lisa. That's because Leonardo vividly illustrates that there is a connection between humanity and nature through the portrait. In the creation of the Mona Lisa, Leonardo combined his scientific knowledge with his artistic talent to produce a work that transcends the boundaries of time and culture."

"There's no doubt that Leonardo da Vinci created a timeless masterpiece in the Mona Lisa." The President interjected.

"The Mona Lisa is not confined to the age of the Renaissance." Abigail expounded.

"Her image echoes through the corridors of time, influencing every era with her timeless beauty and unrivaled mystique. The perfect blend of light and shadow, along with her elusive mystery, causes us to look deeper at the Mona Lisa. She's inviting us to explore, to question, and come in closer. Her influence has permeated every realm of popular culture, from literature to cinema and from music to fashion. The Mona Lisa reminds us that great art is not just about aesthetics but also about sparking curiosity, inspiring creativity, and challenging perspectives. The Mona Lisa has been celebrated in a number of ways, solidifying her status as a cultural icon. She continues to hypnotize, captivate, and mesmerize."

"She had my wife and I mesmerized the other evening. But she's apparently had some practice. The Mona Lisa obviously has been putting people under a spell for centuries." The President remarked.

"Over five hundred years, to be exact, Mr. President." Abigail pointed out.

"The Mona Lisa's name is synonymous with intrigue. Her intimate smile more than hints that she knows something that we don't know. And she desires to share her secrets with those who she trusts. She communicates with her eyes. She speaks to the heart. And her secrets are capturing the world's imagination. There are building blocks that led to the Mona Lisa becoming the most famous portrait of all time. It all began in 1503 in Florence, when Leonardo began painting the Mona Lisa. Leonardo spent the first thirty years of his life in Florence. Afterward, he lived in Milan for twenty years. Then, he returned to Florence. Leonardo began painting the Mona Lisa when he was fifty-one years old. And he took the Mona Lisa with him wherever he went. When King Francois I invited Leonardo to come to France in 1516, he brought the Mona Lisa with him there. Leonardo died three years later in 1519, and the Mona Lisa entered the royal collection at the court of King Francois I and remained there for 250 years. In November of 1799, Napoleon came to power in France. And in 1800, the Mona Lisa was brought to the Tuileries Palace, and placed in the emperor's luxurious bedroom. I really get a gut feeling that the Mona Lisa was not crazy about the idea of being exhibited in Napoleon's bedroom. The French Revolution turned the Louvre in Paris, France, into a museum, which gave the portrait a proper place in the Grand Gallery in 1804. It was on August 21st, 1911, that the Mona Lisa's biggest 'photo opportunity' came. She was stolen, and the story was in newspapers all over the world. Suddenly, the Mona Lisa was an international celebrity. Everyone read the story, knew what she looked like, and wanted to know more about her. The painting was stolen by an Italian handyman by the name of Vincenzo Peruggia, who worked at the Louvre. He believed that the 21-inch x 30-inch Mona Lisa painting rightfully belonged to Italy, not France. He walked out of the museum with the Mona Lisa hidden under his coat. For over two long years, the world's most famous painting was missing, and its whereabouts enthralled the entire globe. Even the famous artist Pablo Picasso was arrested as a suspect and later released. The Mona Lisa was finally recovered in December 1913, after

Peruggia attempted to sell the painting to an Italian art dealer in Florence by the name of Alfred Geri and a museum curator by the name of Giovanni Poggi. The authorities were alerted. Peruggia was arrested immediately by the police and later sentenced to six months in prison. The mystery of the most audacious art theft in history was solved. The Mona Lisa was ceremoniously restored at the Louvre Museum on January 4th, 1914. She was exhibited to massive crowd and protected with a bulletproof case. And the entire story catapulted the Mona Lisa into the limelight as her fame skyrocketed, taking the portrait from being a revered piece of art to a pedestal of becoming a worldwide household name."

"The Mona Lisa deserves that much," the President respectfully commented.

"And, of course, people wonder exactly who the Mona Lisa is. There are a number of theories. The most popular include that she's Isabella d'Este, who was the Marchioness of Mantua; Costanza d'Avalos, who was the Duchess of Francavilla; Lisa Gherardini Del Giocondo, who was an Italian noblewoman and wife of a rich silk merchant, and also the theory that the Mona Lisa is a rendition of Leonardo's mother. None of these theories can be conclusively proven." Abigail mentioned.

"But it was in Florence, a city larger than London, larger than Paris, and larger than Rome, where many creative geniuses gathered. It was a time when everything was under the scrutiny of the church. And yet, at the same time, the church was the main patron who commissioned the artists to do various works."

"Just like Michelangelo was commissioned by the Pope to paint the ceiling of the Sistine Chapel in the Apostolic Palace of the Vatican City in Rome around Leonardo da Vinci's time. They were contemporaries." The President correlated.

"Exactly, President White!" Abigail burst right back into the conversation with enthusiasm.

"Michelangelo and Leonardo da Vinci knew each other. Another vital fact is that sometime after Leonardo had earned his apprenticeship with the renowned Andrea del Verrocchio, there was a two-year undocumented gap in his life. No one knows where he was, what he was doing, or who he was with during these years. He simply disappeared from the historical account. He went on some kind of an excursion, a hiatus. It's been speculated that during these two years, he was tutored by some special individuals, giving him an intimate understanding of nature and the cosmos. One thing is certain. After

Leonardo's return to Florence, his creative output reached a whole new level, going beyond art and extending to numerous other disciplines. He would produce aerial maps of Italian cities with incredible accuracy. He would design and build the world's first self-propelled vehicle. And he would invent machines that were years and even centuries ahead of their time. Somehow, he had developed an incredible burst of creativity. He began to tower above his contemporaries, like Copernicus and Michaelangelo. Many people believe the mystery of Leonardo's two-year disappearance may be found by examining his paintings, especially the Mona Lisa."

"Yes, I remember learning about that mysterious lapse in Leonardo's life." The President recalled.

"Didn't he make a record of that experience in some way?"

"He certainly did, President White! Leonardo made notations in his journals. There is an account where Leonardo details his youthful adventure, describing his encounter with a vast, mysterious cave. Leonardo had been exploring a remote area, searching for inspiration for his art. On this particular day, he wandered through the landscape and stumbled upon this cave that seemed to be calling out to him. He describes being on the edge of this dark cave and said he felt terrified by the darkness of the cave and what might be within it. On the other hand, he showed a desire to try to understand what was in there. It can be safely assumed that this was a very significant event in his life during his disappearance because it made a strong enough impression on him to write it down as one of the few autobiographical notes he ever made. His experience in this cave was important enough for him to incorporate notes about it in his journal. Despite the danger and uncertainty, a bizarre energy drove Leonardo to explore the mysterious cave. He chose to enter the cave 'to see if there was any marvelous thing within.' What he found inside was beyond anything he could have possibly imagined. He is believed to have acquired knowledge way beyond what was conventionally available at that time. The encounter profoundly impacted him. We do know that Leonardo spent a good deal of time in the Apennine Mountains just outside Florence, Italy, when he was young, examining the mysteries of nature. Leonardo traveled for years around the countryside in his youth. He was looking at rocks. He was studying birds. He was observing the flow of water. He was analyzing mountains. Leonardo was literally immersed in nature, and he drew some sort of inspiration from the cave. And after he had ventured into the cave, his works began to radiate mystery and intrigue, far beyond just being an artistic genius. The legend of Leonardo and the cave will live on, never allowing us to stop searching for the truth of what actually happened. No other artist in the Renaissance showed that much interest in the natural world. It's believed that he was in the Apennine Mountains when he discovered the cave. The journal that mentions the cave is Codex Arundel. In the Codex Arundel, Leonardo refers to the cave as 'the cavern of knowledge.' The journal that contains the largest single collection of Leonardo da Vinci's writings is the Codex Atlanticus. There is another journal, the Codex Leicester, which Bill Gates purchased for $30.8 million dollars. Today, there are eleven of Leonardo's codices still surviving that contain thousands of pages."

"That is absolutely incredible, Dr. Grant!" The President exclaimed.

"Yes. It really is amazing. And the results of Leonardo da Vinci's curiosity make it all even more fascinating. His immense genius needed to know answers to big questions. The Boeing AH-64 Apache combat helicopter is a modern-day aerial marvel that would have been impossible to assemble without the designs for vertical flight that were first drawn up by Leonardo da Vinci five-hundred years ago. He invented all the modern weapons that the military is using today. The helicopter, airplane, and submarine were his original concepts. And Leonardo was totally aware that once he had created these weapons of war, even in blueprint form, there was no turning back. He saw the handwriting on the wall. He could vividly depict the wars of the future. Therefore, in 1503, after Leonardo had ceased to invent any more weapons of war, he began the creation of the Mona Lisa to counteract the devastation of what lay ahead for mankind."

"Kind of like cause and effect. Once the wheels were in motion, it was difficult to stop it. But Leonardo found a way! He was that much of a genius." The President reasoned out loud.

"It's difficult to fathom how much of a genius Leonardo da Vinci was, President White!" Abigail emotionally responded.

"If they may have had the technology to match Leonardo's blueprints back when he lived, there's a chance mankind could have landed on the moon in the 1800's. Leonardo is given credit for all the sophisticated robot ideas we have today. At the Leonardo da Vinci Machines Exhibition in St. Louis, Missouri, Italian artists and engineers recreated over sixty of Leonardo's inventions. NASA engineers have developed space technology from his

3D blueprints. Leonardo accomplished a great deal through his extremely high intellectual ability and extraordinary creative range, covering a staggering array of disciplines. He is still influencing science, technology, medicine, art, architecture, and numerous other fields today, over half a millennium after his death. There is a great deal of speculation as to whether there was something more to his intellect than just his genius and creativity. Leonardo didn't just change the world in his lifetime. As human innovation and technology caught up with his ideas, they all worked. His universal quest for knowledge changed the world forever. His contributions to mankind are truly a gift to the world. The answer to exactly where Leonardo da Vinci derived his inspiration lies right before our eyes, in plain sight within the enigmatic smile of a five-hundred-year-old portrait, the Mona Lisa. When the Mona Lisa was painted, she was about twenty-five years old. That's how old Mona Lisa Romano is today. There was a vital reason why Leonardo took the Mona Lisa with him wherever he would go, short of not letting her out of his sight. He was protecting something bigger than the painting itself. Her undeniable, striking, stunning beauty has caused many men who looked upon her to lose their resolve. During the 1800s, many European scholars made reference to her allure, claiming her smile imparted a treacherous attraction, referring to her mocking lips and her gaze that promised unknown pleasures. She has been said to be the very embodiment of timeless, feminine beauty. By the twentieth century, the Mona Lisa was known by many people to be an iconic masterpiece. But her rise to unprecedented fame goes way beyond the canvas itself. In 1550, an Italian scholar, Giorgio Vasari, published a very popular biography of Italian Renaissance artists that was translated and distributed widely, and Leonardo da Vinci's Mona Lisa was included. She is the supreme reflection of the height of the Renaissance. She is filled with secrets waiting to be unraveled, a narrative desiring to be read, and an enigma crying out to be solved. The Mona Lisa is an artistic journey with a map showing the destination of the treasure. Leonardo had an uncanny ability to capture the essence of the subjects that he painted. He breathed life into them through his style of artistry. This is quite evident in his most famous painting, the Mona Lisa. This is why she is the most recognized and studied piece of art in the world. The secrets of our future and our fate may very well be found in the work of Leonardo da Vinci. He was the ultimate Renaissance man, the standard bearer. He possessed the most brilliant mind the world has ever known. Leonardo is using the image of the Mona Lisa as a key to crack the code that spans the range of his life's work. The background of the Mona Lisa looks like a beautiful nature scene. But when you observe closer, the water is clearly higher on the right side than the water on the left side, as though a flood is inevitable. If we remove the figure of the Mona Lisa from the picture, the waters come crashing together. The Mona Lisa is preventing the flood. Taking her out of the painting will cause a deluge and severe flood of the water. The only thing that is stopping the inevitable flood is the Mona Lisa. Leonardo, through the Mona Lisa, is conveying feelings, emotions, and expressions of nature, as well as the human being. This changes the Mona Lisa into the most immortal image of all time. Herein lies the meaning of why the Mona Lisa is so special. Leonardo thought in terms of time and nature in cycles. Where most people see chaos, Leonardo saw rhythms, patterns, and cycles. It is quite possible that he drew on his observation of natural disasters to predict future catastrophes. He foresaw a time when human beings and their technology would begin to have a devastating effect on the natural world. He knew that the weapons that would be developed in the future would exceed the maturity of mankind. Leonardo was not saying that nature needs to be overcome. He was saying that nature is something we need to live in sync with. Leonardo is urging mankind not to deplete the Earth's natural resources, not to create weapons of mass destruction that destroy human beings and nature, and not to cause problems that harm our environment by creating a lack of climate control. The Mona Lisa states that mankind is utilizing destructive power to destroy nature, and caution must be taken to stop it. Leonardo's hope was that his ideas would develop in the future to bring nothing but good to the human race. And improve our quality of life."

"It's a probability that Leonardo da Vinci's intention, through the creation of the Mona Lisa, was to thrust world peace upon us all, whether the human race wants it or not!" President White thoughtfully and carefully surmised.

"Leonardo could very well be even more of a genius than we've given him credit for."

"That's why Leonardo would not let the Mona Lisa out of his sight, President White. That's why he took the portrait everywhere he went. Whether it was intentional or he stumbled into painting the Mona Lisa, at some point, he knew that she was something very special. And now, Leonardo is speaking to us beyond the grave through the Mona Lisa. While the apocalypse is, in general, being foreseen by Leonardo, the flood waters of the Mona Lisa portrait are not predicting Armageddon by the waters of a great flood that will engulf the earth. Leonardo da Vinci knew both the Old and New Testaments of the Bible, and he was fully aware of the promise being made that the Earth would never again be destroyed by a flood. Leonardo wanted to make it clear that the human race is doing harm to our natural surroundings and all of these current-day factors that are putting mankind at risk could be prevented by a sweet, dear lady who we fondly refer to as the Mona Lisa. She is very concerned about the order of nature where humanity is concerned. The Mona Lisa should not be misinterpreted as Leonardo's indication that Armageddon is coming. The message he's conveying through the Mona Lisa is that Armageddon doesn't have to occur at all! It can be prevented, if mankind will simply stop long enough to heed what nature is attempting to communicate. Leonardo da Vinci created the Mona Lisa to be the center of the universe. The Mona Lisa is the missing link! Mr. President, Leonardo da Vinci was not attempting to predict the apocalypse. He was desiring to prevent the apocalypse through the influence of the Mona Lisa!"

"And you feel that Mona Romano is involved in seeing this situation played out, Dr. Grant?" The President enquired forthrightly.

"Yes, I do, Mr. President. There's no doubt about it. I know what I've witnessed. Mona is involved by no choice of her own. And whether she is chosen to be your next National Security Advisor or not, she will continue to be involved either way. For that matter, I'm involved as well, very deeply." Abigail said firmly.

"I'm beginning to get the sensation that I'm involved with this riddle myself." The President confessed.

"In fact, after everything that's happened, along with the perspective that you've just provided, it's safe to say that I'm in deep."

"I would be inclined to agree with you, Mr. President," Abigail affirmed.

The President paused for several seconds in serious contemplation.

"Dr. Grant, under the circumstances, I think it would be a travesty for me not to be considerate enough to invite you to a viewing of the Mona Lisa, especially after you made such a long trip from New York to the White House." The President said cordially.

"And especially since the Mona Lisa has had such a long journey from Paris, France. Of course, it's history in the making by having the Mona Lisa in the White House."

The Mona Lisa Portrait in The East Room of The White House

"Yes, sir. I thought you'd never ask, Mr. President," Abigail responded with a genuine smile of appreciation. "That would be exciting!"

It wasn't long before the President and Abigail were together in the East Room of the White House, standing directly in front of the Mona Lisa. And it was apparent by the expression on the President's face that he once again was overwhelmed with intrigue by the presence of the

Mona Lisa, especially being privy to the fresh information that Abigail had just shared with him.

"It's just like you had mentioned, Dr. Grant. She communicates with her eyes." The President said, completely mesmerized by the Mona Lisa.

"Yes. And metaphysically as well. She speaks to the heart in a very powerful manner." Abigail elaborated.

"I can safely deduce, President White, that the Mona Lisa derives great joy out of being in the White House before it's her time to go back to the Louvre Museum in Paris."

"And we can both rest in the fact that Mona Romana has been a faithful viewer of the Mona Lisa during her stay here in the East Room of the White House." The President could not resist pointing it out.

"That's a given, President White," Abigail confirmed.

"Dr. Grant, please do me a big favor. Would you let Mona know that I would be very pleased to have her as my next National Security Advisor?" The President could not have sounded any more sincere.

"I don't think that it will be secondhand news coming from you."

"I'd be happy to, Mr. President!" Abigail responded. "There's just one thing that I might mention, though."

"What's that, Dr. Grant?" The President asked.

"This may not be the last time that you summon me to the White House with questions concerning Mona," Abigail predicted.

"Oh, I have little doubt about that, Dr. Grant." The President of the United States concurred.

"I honestly get the sensation that Mona Lisa Romano knows something that we don't know, and, of course, I mean that in a good way."

"That's exactly what they say about the Mona Lisa in the portrait before us, Mr. President. Perhaps one day, we'll discover just what that secret may be." Abigail conjected.

9

The media and the American people were all somewhat surprised by President White's choice for his new National Security Advisor compared to the other potential candidates, who seemed to possess all the required credentials, qualifications, and necessary experience. Mona Lisa Romano had, by way of comparison, served in the National Security Council as Executive Secretary for a relatively brief period. And some on Capitol Hill, even though they would not be voting on the National Security Council position, felt that Mona stood out as someone who was a novice who would have to prove her effectiveness as National Security Advisor. Mona had already demonstrated herself in Washington as a knowledgeable policy advisor, and with the power of her disarming charm, she had established positive friendships with many influential people in the Capital city of Washinton, D.C. But there were critics who thought it was unheard of that the President had selected a relatively unknown, twenty-five-year-old, who they claimed was too inexperienced.

President White chose to introduce Mona Lisa Romano to the American public himself via television with the Washington, D.C. logo in white letters on a blue wall directly behind the National Security Council team, who were positioned to the rear of the President and Mona. Everyone was practically standing at attention.

"Mona Lisa Romano's accomplishments in the field of international affairs more than qualify her for the position of National Security Advisor." President White justified to all of America.

"She has been an exemplary model as Executive Secretary with the National Security Council, serving as the best kind of statesperson that can be found anywhere. She's worked with the State Department and Secretary of State Cameron Quinn. She has contributed to the significant role of developing pertinent foreign policy in various parts of the world. She has served as a lead negotiator in talks that resulted in nuclear deals and ceasefires, calling on nations, including the United States, to lay down arms. She attended a first-class university, New York University, better known as NYU, graduating at the top of her class as an undergraduate and as a postgraduate student, earning both her Master's Degree and Ph.D., also at NYU. Mona has been active for National Security Action, which advocates progressive American leadership. While there are some who consider Dr. Romano too young for the position of National Security Advisor, there are many more who are

162

confident that her boundless energy will capture the imaginations of our young people in the United States and perhaps even young people around the world. While the difference of strong views can be quite a challenge at the negotiating table, Mona has found herself in a number of situations where she has had to respond quickly and decisively in negotiations on behalf of the United States, and her record of decision-making has been right on target. She is aware of the most difficult operation issues around the world, and her sound advice regarding the resolution of these issues is not only valuable to me but also valuable to all those within the sound of my voice. She has shown the capability of effective leadership at National Security Council meetings in evaluating each one of these precarious situations with all of their particular complex components. Dr. Romano and the National Security Council, on a daily basis, will be instrumental in helping me figure out the best foreign policy options that need to be considered and then oversee the process of appropriately implementing these policies. It is a great joy for me to present to the American people our current National Security Advisor, Dr. Mona Lisa Romano."

"Thank you, Mr. President," Mona responded, smiling after she reached the podium to look straight into the television camera at the American public.

"Thank you for that most generous introduction. For a National Security Advisor to be effective, he or she must have a solid foundation in international affairs, matters of national defense, and political science. Acquiring serious experience by working with various government departments like the Department of State, the Department of Defense, and other governmental agencies allows a formidable National Security Advisor to be even more productive, as he or she has had a good deal of exposure to policy-making and strategic planning. And I am thankful that we, as a nation, have a President who desires to be vitally engaged in foreign policy. During President John F. Kennedy's Administration, the National Security Council staff consisted of five members. Today, there are a total number of twelve people on the National Security Council team, between the Statutory Members and Statutory Advisors, chaired by President White.

JFK With His National Security Council

We are confronted by many national security issues, which are scrutinized in the West Wing of the White House. A National Security Council meeting may be called for any number of reasons, especially at the urging of the President, and many times, these meetings are called on account of some sort of crisis. We are confident that the policies that we develop at the White House will smoothly carry over to the negotiating tables for future summits that have already been scheduled to elevate our partnership with many nations around the world. As the President and I head to the next World Summit, we are committed to illustrating to the countries who are represented that the world's economies can all work together, even in these challenging times. We feel that the United States is bringing a lot of benefits to the table at this upcoming summit. Of course, we feel that the efforts made at this summit will work to build our American economy as well. We are, indeed, committed to these nations and desire to assist them with any difficulty that they may face. We will keep the American public completely informed, with all transparency, concerning any and all developing economic global partnerships and increasing World Bank financing. We believe this multilateral approach will boost the welfare and productivity of all countries concerned. The United States is encouraging all nations of our world to acknowledge that our current economic global dilemma must be resolved collectively. Based on this awareness, we cannot fail to design creative solutions that we all may agree upon in working united toward a meaningful, prosperous outcome."

And so, Mona Lisa was officially introduced to everyone as President Alexander H. White's new National Security Advisor. Mona was all of a sudden right on the cutting edge, working hard, fast, and continuously to build good diplomatic relations.

The National Security Advisor (NSA) offers the President a wide range of options on national security issues. Mona Lisa Romano's duties as National Security Advisor included helping to plan the President's foreign travel, providing memos and staffing for the President's meetings, and securing communications with world leaders. Air Force One, carrying the President, Mona Lisa Romano, and their entourage, taxied the runway for the World Summit in Geneva, Switzerland. This meeting among leaders of the world's largest economies came at a time of increasing geopolitical divisions. Notably, both Chinese President Enchen Yang and Russian President Igor Ivanov would not be present at this year's World Summit hosted by Switzerland. One White House official described the meeting as an Earth-shaking corridor. One of the big goals for the President at this summit was to bolster the ability for alternative lending to developing countries. The President was specifically trying to improve institutions like the World Bank and the International Monetary Fund in their ability to assist these countries. But President White and National Security Advisor Mona Lisa Romano had their work cut out for them, attempting to leverage the U.S. commitment by getting other Western allies to participate. Yet, despite all the apparent obstacles, President White and his new National Security Advisor managed to get a great deal accomplished. They proved themselves to be a productive team, identifying and tackling challenges, taking advantage of good opportunities, solving problems, and generating creative ideas. President White and Mona defied the odds, employing a number of economic policies that would be quite mutually beneficial for many countries.

And from this point on, Mona Lisa was off to the races. With or without the President, no matter where she went, her boundless energy went with her. She chaired meetings of the Principals Committee of the National Security Council herself when the President wasn't present, which included United States Secretary of State, Cameron Quinn, the Deputy Secretary at the State Department, Romeo Barone, who came from time to time, and the Secretary of Defense, Kenneth R. Urban. Other regular attendees included the Vice President, Richard O. Green; the Secretary of the Treasury, Greg Johnston; the Secretary of Energy, William Brackner; the Attorney General, Kip Sharpe; the Secretary of Homeland Security, Jon T. Wells; the Representative of the United States of America to the United Nations, Jerry Morris, the Administrator of the U.S. Agency for Internal Development, Joe Bettinger, the Chief of Staff to the President, Mark Mann, the Assistant to the President for National Security Affairs, John Chowilla, the Chairman of the Joint Chiefs of Staff, Tommy Beale, the Director of

National Intelligence, Leland Davis, Counsel to the President, Monie Brunson, and Legal Advisor to the National Security Council, Barbara Thompson. The heads of other executive departments and agencies, as well as other senior officials, were also invited to attend NSC meetings to cover many critical national security issues, such as global public health, international economics, climate control, science and technology, cybersecurity, migration, and other priority topics.

Mona was also attending State Department meetings that included the Secretary of State, Cameron Quinn, Deputy Secretary, Romeo Barone, NATO Secretary-General, Daniel Van Meter, and Secretary of Defense, Kenneth R. Urban.

Not all United States Presidents in the past have allowed their National Security Advisor to participate at the Cabinet table with his other advisors, but President Alexander White would not hear of Mona not being allowed to sit in on his Cabinet meetings. Mona's input was just too important to him.

As National Security Advisor, in the course of several years, she traveled to a staggering number of 146 different countries around the world, employing diplomacy, implementing foreign policies, and negotiating for the human rights of people of all nations. And wherever Mona went, she always left the indelible mark of her charm. She always left behind a genuine feeling of warmth that rendered the impression that the United States really cared about the people that they were reaching out to. No matter where Mona Lisa Romano went, people never forgot her. She became known as the champion of world freedom. And everyone on the planet knew who Mona was. Mona Lisa became loved by a following of many, many people on Earth. Mona could be seen on television on the news forums, "Face the Nation" on CBS with moderator Debra Davis, and on "Meet the Press" on NBC with moderator Nora O'Hara on Sunday mornings. In fact, Mona could be seen discussing international matters on various news broadcasts all over the world. She held regular press conferences at the White House and out in the field to ensure that the media and the American public were always informed and up to date on pertinent global matters. Mona Lisa Romano demonstrated herself to be one of the greatest communicators that America had ever witnessed. And she worked tirelessly to reduce hostile tensions in the world, no matter where the stress may be. People were astonished and mystified to witness this sweet, petite, unassuming, amiable young lady so gracefully perform her assignment of diplomacy in the face of such horrific danger. People were absolutely intrigued with United States National Security Advisor, Mona Lisa Romano.

10

Close to the two-year mark when President Alexander Hampton White would be going out of office at the end of his second term, Alexander White's Administration was facing yet another major national security decision: Who would be the next United States Secretary of State? Due to health issues, the beloved Secretary of State, Cameron Quinn, was forced by insistent doctors to take an indefinite leave of absence.

The United States Secretary of State is the President's chief foreign affairs advisor. As the highest-ranking member of the President's Cabinet, the office holder of Secretary of State is the third-highest official of the Executive Branch of the U.S. Federal government, after the President and the Vice President. The Secretary of State is fourth in line to succeed the Presidency, after the Speaker of the House. The Secretary of State, along with the Secretary of the Treasury, the Secretary of Defense, and the Attorney General, are regarded as the four most crucial Cabinet members due to the importance of their respective departments.

The United States Secretary of State carries out the President's foreign policies through the State Department and the Foreign Service of the United States. The Secretary of State is nominated by the President and, following a confirmation hearing before the Senate Committee of Foreign Relations, must be confirmed by a majority vote by the United States Senate, consisting of 100 Senators.

Created in 1789, with Thomas Jefferson as the first United States Secretary of State, the office represents the United States to foreign nations. Other prior United States Secretary of States include James Madison, James Monroe, John Quincy Adams, James Buchanan, Henry Clay, Daniel Webster, William Seward, Edward Everett, Henry Kissinger, Edmund Muskie, Alexander Haig and George Schultz (both under the Administration of President Ronald Wilson Reagan), Condoleezza Rice, General Colin L. Powell, Hillary Clinton, John Kerry, Rex Tillerson, Michael Pompeo, and Antony Blinken. The stated duties of the Secretary of State are to supervise the United States foreign service and immigration policy and to administer the U.S. Department of State. The United States Secretary of State must also advise the President on U.S. foreign matters, such as the appointment of diplomats and ambassadors. The United States Secretary of State conducts negotiations and has the power to interpret and terminate treaties relating to foreign policy. The Secretary of State also participates in international conferences, organizations, and agencies as a representative of the United States. The Secretary of State communicates issues relating to United States foreign policy to Congress and U.S. citizens. The Secretary of State provides services to U.S. citizens living or traveling abroad, such as providing credentials in the form of passports. By doing this, the United States Secretary of State ensures the protection of citizens, their property, and interests in foreign countries. The United States Secretary of State has domestic responsibilities as well in the United States, such as the performance of protocol functions that take place in the White House. Congress may occasionally add to the responsibilities of the United States Secretary of State.

As popular as Mona Lisa Romano had become as National Security Advisor, directly responsible for the administrative duties performed by the National Security Council and reporting to the President of the United States, it was apparent to everyone that Mona would be a viable candidate for the office of United States Secretary of State. And that's exactly what happened. The President nominated Mona Lisa to become America's next United States Secretary of State. It went to the Senate Committee on Foreign Relations, which conducted a confirmation hearing, and it was confirmed by a vote in the Senate with a majority of 100 to 0. Mona Lisa Romano was the only person in U.S. history to be appointed unanimously to the office of United States Secretary of State, other than General Colin L. Powell under President George W. Bush.

The day following Mona Lisa Romano's confirmation as United States Secretary of State, a press conference was held at the State Department. The room was filled with journalists from around the world, eager to hear from the newly appointed Secretary.

As Mona approached the steps of the State Department, she was getting goosebumps from the stark realization that it would not have been possible for Mona Lisa, to become the United States Secretary of State without the devoted influence and protective care of Dr. Abigail Grant, coupled with the fact that Leonardo da Vinci's Mona Lisa, who Mona Lisa Romano had been named after, had always been working behind the scenes. Abigail had constantly been there for Mona, and for that matter, so had the Mona Lisa. On this momentous occasion, Mona's mind became flooded with personable memories that she collectively shared with Abigail. And Mona could surely sense her metaphysical connection with the Mona Lisa was stronger than ever. And now, Mona walked the hallways of the State Department building that she had been in so many times before, with the new perspective that she was now the head of the State Department.

Mona stepped up to the podium, her presence commanding the room. Cameras flashed as she smiled confidently, looking out at the sea of reporters.

"Good afternoon, everyone," Mona began. "It is an immense honor and privilege to stand before you today as the newly appointed United States Secretary of State. I want to express my deepest gratitude to President Alexander Hampton White for his unwavering trust and support and to the Senate for their unanimous confirmation. This moment is a testament to the collaborative efforts of countless individuals dedicated to the service of our great nation."

She paused, allowing her words to resonate. "As Secretary of State, I am committed to advancing our nation's foreign policy objectives, promoting peace, and fostering international cooperation. Our world faces numerous challenges, from climate change to cybersecurity threats, and it is imperative that we address these issues with innovation, empathy, and unwavering resolve."

Mona continued, outlining her vision for the State Department. "We will focus on strengthening our alliances, building new partnerships, and enhancing our diplomatic efforts globally. I believe in the power of diplomacy and the importance of dialogue in resolving conflicts and creating a more secure and prosperous world."

A reporter from the Washington Post raised his hand. "Madam Secretary, what will be your immediate priorities as you step into this new role?"

"Thank you for your question," Mona replied.

"My immediate priorities include addressing the ongoing conflicts in various regions, working toward sustainable solutions for climate change, and bolstering our cybersecurity measures. Additionally, I aim to prioritize human rights and democracy, ensuring that our foreign policy reflects the values we hold dear as a nation."

Another reporter, this time from the BBC, asked, "Secretary Romano, how do you plan to navigate the current tensions between the United States and other global powers?"

Mona nodded thoughtfully. "Navigating international tensions requires a balanced approach of firmness and diplomacy. We will engage in constructive dialogues with our allies and adversaries alike, seeking common ground while standing firm on our principles. It's essential to foster mutual understanding and cooperation to address global challenges effectively."

As the press conference drew to a close, Mona took a moment to reflect. "I am deeply aware of the responsibilities that come with this position, and I am ready to tackle them head-on with dedication and integrity. Together, we will work toward a brighter, more peaceful future for all."

With that, she stepped away from the podium, greeted by applause from the audience. The press conference had set a tone of optimism and determination for her tenure as Secretary of State.

Once again, Mona had made a viable connection with the media and dazzled the world with her disarming charm. Mona Lisa Romano was now officially America's sweetheart.

The State Department, Washington, D.C.

Mona was sitting at her new desk at the State Department on her first day as United States Secretary of State, attempting to get everything organized.

Then, she realized that someone was silently standing at the doorway of her office. Mona looked up, trying not to appear startled. It was her Deputy Secretary who would serve as her right-hand man at the State Department.

"Looks like the world is raging out of control, Dr. Romano," Romeo Barone remarked.

Mona knew Romeo indirectly, having worked closely with the previous Secretary of State, Cameron Quinn. The former Secretary of State had brought the Deputy Secretary to National Security Council meetings on occasion. Romeo had a distinct, imposing presence about him, being six feet tall, with curly black hair, brown eyes, and prominent cheekbones. And Romeo, at age thirty-five, was five years older than Mona.

"Well, that ensures a lot of job security for a United States Secretary of State. And call me Mona, Romeo," Mona Lisa insisted. Mona knew that Romeo was a colorful character.

"Ah, a sense of humor!" Romeo couldn't help but notice.

"I'm just attempting to add a little levity to the situation," Mona retorted.

"Well, all's fair in love and war, Mona. Although, between the two, I tend to think there's more fair in war."

"Ah, a sense of humor!" Mona responded, sitting behind her desk with an expression on her face like she was genuinely tickled. The rapport between Romeo and Mona as two future comrades in arms was instantly established.

"Sense of humor runs in my family," Romeo asserted.

"I like your family name," Mona confessed.

"Oh, really. Why's that?" Romeo sincerely enquired.

"Because it's Italian, Romeo Barone!" Mona said, with a very pleased smile on her face.

"Oh, yeah. Being Italian runs in the family, too. Looks like we have something in common. You can't have a last name more Italian than Romano," Romeo pointed out.

"Well, thank you, Romeo. What higher praise! I'm glad you noticed. I will certainly take that as a compliment," Mona said, continuing to maintain her glowing smile.

Mona and Romeo worked hard together to plant the seeds of peace in the world. The coordinated efforts of the United States State Department had never been more in sync. Despite the tremendous pressure that the adored United States Secretary of State Mona Lisa Romano was under, she always appeared poised and beautiful to the American public. Mona Lisa, Romeo, and their entourage traveled to many countries to create closer and closer relationships of goodwill and prosperity among nations, with the blessing of the President of the United States, Alexander Hampton White.

CBS NEWS UNITED STATES

STATE DEPARTMENT WORLDWIDE REPORT

"We interrupt this broadcast to bring you a live Special Report. Here is CBS News Chief White House and State Department Correspondent, Devon Walsh, reporting from the United States Department of State Daily Press Briefing

Room: "United States Secretary of State Mona Romano is just about to provide details of a massive multilateral hostage exchange that has come as a result of numerous behind closed doors negotiations that have been going on for an unspecified amount of time." Devon Walsh stated to open her report. "These undisclosed talks have been taking place on top of the open summits which have been routinely covered by the Press. Secretary of State Romano, who has described herself as an advocate of transparency to the American people, has clearly stated that it is now the appropriate moment to share the apparent positive outcome of these secretive meetings. Behind me now here at the Department of State Daily Press Briefing Room, State Department Press Briefing Spokesman, Jeremiah Denton, Jr., is taking questions from the media prior to United States Secretary of State Romano addressing these unprecedented developments. President White has obviously been vitally involved in these covert meetings with numerous world leaders and diplomats, and we have learned that after Secretary of State Romano speaks here today, she and her negotiating team, including State Department Deputy Secretary Romeo Barone, will immediately be resuming further negotiations to insure the freedom of yet more hostages, on top of the hundreds of hostages whose freedom has already been secured at this time. CBS News has learned that certain families of released hostages have met with President White in the Oval Office of the White House. This is an absolutely unprecedented, extraordinary development on the part of the State Department and their colleagues. Jeremiah Denton, Jr. has concluded making his announcements and answering preliminary questions. He is now bringing United States Secretary of State Romano to the podium. And here she is now."

STATE DEPARTMENT DAILY PRESS BEIEFING ROOM

Mona Lisa approached the podium with poise and great dignity before the standing room only Daily Press Briefing Room at the State Department. Mona was totally collective, despite her intense involvement over an extended period of time of negotiations and detailed diplomatic matters orchestrated and directed by President White, herself, and Romeo Barone, her Deputy Secretary. With the www.STATE.GOV logos flanked by the American and State Department flags behind her, and the Department of State seal on the podium in front of her, Mona became the focal point of attention as she addressed America and the world.

"Thank you, Jeremiah. And good afternoon, everyone." Mona said to open the Press Conference. "As a result of the culmination of a monumental level of effort and the exercising of a high standard of communication skill by my colleagues across the national security enterprise, including my negotiating team here at the State Department, my colleagues at the National Security Council, and my colleagues at the Central Intelligence Agency. I am happy to announce that an intricate and expansive deal has been secured unlike anything of its kind in history in regard to people who have been held hostage all around the world and cease fires that have taken place in many regions as a direct result. These have been complex incidences that have fortunately yielded a positive resolution. Hundreds of hostages around the entire world, who have been separated from their loved ones, are right now in preparation to be reunited with their families and friends. President White and our negotiating team have been dedicated to high-pressure, highest-level international crisis negotiations. There have been many, many layers of emotional complexity regarding these talks, and it has required the refined expertise of everyone involved with this imperative effort. This allegiance of talented professionals have not been in it for the photo opp. At President White's direction, they have acted on behalf of the American people in conjunction with leaders and diplomats from many nations as a well-oiled machine, willing to sacrifice their lives so that others may be set free. They are to be saluted. And every American in the United States should be thankful to have people of such commendable character standing in the gap on behalf of our country's national security."

Mona Lisa pointed to Bob Tatom, CNN's outstanding United States State Department correspondent, who motioned with his hand.

"Can you give us an update on the hostage talks and the potential for an overall ceasefire?" Bob asked politely.

"A worldwide, overall cease fire is on the table today, as we speak, which we are earnestly working toward in conjunction to realizing the release of all remaining hostages. We are insisting that there be utter regard for human lives. We are also looking for greater and greater opportunities to fly humanitarian assistance in for those who have been afflicted in war-torn regions of the world. We are going to continually stay at the negotiating tables and remain engaged until we see the big picture deal accomplished." Mona revealed. "The President has been making ongoing phone calls to world leaders to move this massive proposal along. He has been personally participating in many of the covert summit meetings. This is an open door that we could not ignore or allow to close. We are determined to generate a worldwide ceasefire for the sake of humanity and build on that to promote an enduring peace among the nations of Earth. At this conjure, we are cautiously optimistic. And as we press upon all nations, including those representing terrorist groups, to do their part to help deliver this overall ceasefire, it is incumbent of all people around the world to allow their voices to be heard for a desire of freedom and peace. And in the days to come, I will be able to speak in even greater definition."

"Do you have an estimate of the total number of hostages that remain captive worldwide?" ABC State Department correspondent, Cynthia Mona, enquired.

"We've been straightforward about this, Cynthia," Mona asserted, "as have other countries that are negotiating hostage releases, that we do not know the exact number of hostages overall who are alive at this time. We do know where the vast majority of hostages are being held, but we won't know the exact number of hostages until they are all safely in the hands of authorities and in the arms of their families. Obviously, we are referring to many people being detained or held hostage, so this entails a monumental effort. We are adamant to stop violations of international laws of war, taking civilians as human shields, using hospitals and other institutions for military purposes such a command centers and places to store weapons or house terrorists. We do not want to see innocent lives caught in the crossfire. The loss of a single innocent life is a tragedy, no matter what their nationality may happen to be. We believe in the sanctity of life, and we genuinely grief for the suffering these remaining hostages are having to endure. We've been using our diplomacy to rally many countries. I can assure you that being so close to this unprecedented goal, we will not rest until every last hostage is restored to their loved ones. You can count on our relentless dedication to see this extremely serious objective through to term."

"Mona, do you have any concern that the United States publicly negotiating a hostage release with terrorists on such a large scale will send a message that will ultimately put the lives of other Americans at risk on the world stage?" NBC State Department correspondent, Nora O'Hara, posed.

"Nora, that is a very valid question. We have been working closely with President White since the beginning of his Administration in taking steps to bring hostages home, whether they be American or any other nationality. These are people who have been unjustly detained or being held hostage overseas under various circumstances. And we have been willing to make many hard decisions to accomplish that, especially in regard to hostages who are being brutally held by terrorist groups. While the President has stated all along that his number one priority is to bring hostages home, the strict policy approach that we abide by when negotiating with nations advocating dangerous terrorist groups is complied with to the letter. We do not exceed any boundaries that would cause other Americans, or anyone else for that matter, to find themselves in harm's way. We are going to use every resource in our power, utilizing diplomacy, influence, leverage, with a certain degree of wisdom, to get these people home safely to their families and friends, without endangering anyone else in the course of this process. That is the commitment of President White, that is my personal commitment, and that is the commitment of all of my colleagues."

"Mona, whose idea was it to bring so many hostages home at one time rather than pursuing a one-by-one hostage deal?" Asked by Chief MSNBC News State Department correspondent, Jill Reed.

"Jill, I believe it's safe to say that if we did not have a United States President with the vision and strength that President Alexander Hampton White possesses, these events would never have happened." Mona Lisa firmly responded. "The President has led vigorously and demonstrated himself to be a dynamic, fearless, innovative, charismatic, influential Commander-in-Chief. Of course, there were many people who played a central role in achieving this level of coordination together to allow everything to fall into place. This has been the direct result of a phenomenal team effort. While it has been necessary that certain sensitive channels around the world be protected, many relationships of respect and friendship have been established during this fateful process. President White was determined to get this done, and there were many people under his direction who followed suit, completely confident in his leadership and what he desired to see accomplished, despite any and all obstacles that stood in our way."

Jill Reed quickly responded with another question. "The collaborative effort of securing the release of so many hostages to all the countries respectively must have required some special, unique strategies on the part of your negotiating them to make this massive effort possible. I know magicians are hesitant to share their methods of magic because it is considered a core principle of the art, but do you feel free to reveal any special approach and course of action used at the negotiating tables that the President and your diplomats may have employed to cause all this to work so effectively?"

"Yes, Jill. Under the circumstances, I feel that's a very fair question." Mona responded graciously. "Of course, everyone in the room is aware that my diplomatic code is one of transparency. And the American public is entitled to know the details of just how these results came about. We have exercised great patience to learn what the other countries wanted. We did not engage until we first identified the situation that we were getting into, seeking to understand the points of view of those on the other side of the negotiating table. We listened carefully to their objectives. We asked the important questions first in an attempt to get on the same page. It was a collective, gallant effort to seek out common ground that we could mutually work on. We were very tactful with our timing of expressing our intentions in order to achieve the greatest impact. We established a certain degree of rapport. And at the first opportune moment, and only then, we effectively prepared them to become receptive to our wishes. We demonstrated ourselves to be active listeners, which allowed us to steer the conversations and become problem solvers. We were successful at reflecting back any and all of the worthy statements that they brought up. We managed to get behind the emotions of their pertinent remarks. We reinforced their contributions when we felt that progress was being made. And we intentionally paused for effect in our dialogues, leaving them open to keep talking. We demonstrated to those on the other side of the negotiating table that we understood them, by summarizing and emphasizing all of their positive comments. We actively listened for the purpose of making them feel that they were making a great contribution to a cause that would benefit them as well. And our negotiating team painstakingly did all of this out of empathy and compassion for the hostages whose lives were at stake. We were not only careful concerning the words we chose to say, but we were most deliberate in how we expressed these words. We were even mindful of our body language. To a certain extent, we exercised the power of respect, despite our differences in outlook. In these critical moments, it was imperative that we had the power to be impactful. Once we got their undivided attention, we could assure them that our intentions were honorable and dispel any clouds of suspicion. We managed to get them to a place where they could hear us. And we knew exactly when to express our desires. We were determined to overcome the issues with reasonable rebuttals to objections. We took an approach that gave us the latitude to minimize any mistakes in the negotiation process. We addressed everyone with dignity, in a noble attempt to rise above adversity and get our hostages to a place of safety where they belong. We stayed in a positive frame of mind, which assisted in acquiring spontaneous reactions at the negotiation tables. Very fortunately, we reached a peaceful surrender of the hostages, which has served to better our world and bring great relief to many family members of the hostages who have been freed. We exercised the policy to trust but verify. United Nations delegates will be going to these respective countries to ensure that these agreements will be smoothly carried out. And another important stipulation of the deal resulting from these talks is that the Red Cross will be allowed to go in and access all the remaining hostages who need medical care. The Red Cross will also be allowed to gather data concerning the condition of the remainder of these hostages. These hostages are not forgotten. We are determined to get all of these hostages out of the brutal conditions that they have been subjected to. We are fighting for them. We are working day and night to bring them home. They are the very heartbeat of the bipartisan strides that the United States Congress is making. We are calling for the release of the remainder of these hostages, and we will not slow our pace in this endeavor. We need to draw upon our clarity, consistency, and firmness to bring hope to these remaining hostages and put an end to the wars that made them captive. The United States is taking a stand against oppression wherever it may arise, and we are using all our power and resources bring an end to it."

"Mona, this is a day of great celebration in American history! Can you take a moment to describe the scene with the families of the hostages who were present with the President in the Oval Office of the White House?" Devon

Walsh, CBS News Chief White House and State Department correspondent, requested.

"Yes. It is, indeed, a beautiful day, Devon! And I'd be more than happy to elaborate on the wonderful scene that manifested in the Oval Office." Mona responded, with an exuberant expression of joy on her face, appearing to fight back her tears. "It was the single most emotional event that I have ever been a part of. President White invited the families of the members who had been detained and held hostage at the very moment we received word that all the expected exchanges were complete. And it was President White who told the families that their respective family members were safe. Other families around the world have been contacted by concerned individuals designated to bring it to their attention that their relatives, who were once captive, are now in good hands. The President has also been making calls to other families to personally inform them that their family members who have been held hostage are now rescued. Once again, I must emphasize that witnessing the family's reactions in the Oval Office after President White personally informed them that their loved ones were safe was the most moving scene that I have ever experienced. The joy that radiated from the Oval Office was palpable. And the tears that were shed represented an ocean of love and an entire universe of relief."

"Mona, can you please give us your assessment of just how hot the world temperature is right now and how great the risks are of an all-out World War?" Donald Parks of CNN News asked.

"We have had laser beam focus on preventing the escalation of a World War." Mona Lisa began. "There have been quite a few moments that have required intensive effort to keep things contained at the status quo and maintain a strong current state of affairs. And especially with the presence of Weapons of Mass Destruction in our world, the risk has always been there. And the risk remains today. We believe that we have to continue to be vitally engaged now in ongoing concentrated efforts, through deterrence, through de-escalation, and through diplomatic relations to prevent a full-scale war from taking place. And we will continue to do that. We're, obviously, working very closely with NATO, with our allies, and all of our partners to insure that our security is going to be strong, resilient, and credible no matter what may happen next. But we do remain available to engage more and more in arms control discussions, as the United States did with the Soviet Union at the height of the Cold War."

"Mona, when can we expect to see the last of the U.S. hostages arrive on American soil?" Nora O'Hara, NBC Chief Correspondent at the State Department asked, for her second question.

"It's safe to say, Nora, that we may expect all the American hostages, after going through necessary channels, back on American soil and reunited with their loved ones within two weeks from today, for the most part." Mona pointed out. "The only exceptions would be for those hostages who are under a doctor's care in a hospital of another country. After their respective medical recoveries, they will all be safely transferred to the United States."

"Can you tell us exactly where things stand on the latest hostage negotiations regarding the remainder of the hostages? Is there any real progress being made yet? Are both sides making the kind of concessions that are going to be necessary for success?" Deryl Pendleton, FOX State Department correspondent, asked.

"Yes, Deryl." Mona quickly responded. "We have seen many countries take steps forward in terms of what they are putting on the table. At the very least, we are seeking to cease the harsh conditions that these hostages have suffered, and the President is prepared to impose a sweeping set of sanctions to send a clear message on exactly where the United States stands on this priority issue. As a result of the hostages who have been freed, a policy enforcing ceasefires is being honored by many nations, and this is serving to make the way clear for the remaining hostages to be freed as well. This is a palpable development. There will continue to be further discussions to hammer out the details. And we have high hopes that in soon coming days there will be a firm and final agreement on all fronts. The position of the United States is clear. We would like to see this deal accomplished. We would like to see every last hostage restored to their families. And we would like to see cease fires on all fronts for the safety of innocent children and civilians. And the United States, President White, the State Department, my colleagues, and our allies will do everything in our power to secure a multilateral agreement to this effect."

"Is it your expectation that the pause in the fighting in the Middle East will extend to a lasting peace?" Jennifer Wells, FOX News State Department head correspondent asked.

"Jennifer, all the cards have been laid on the negotiating table in the Middle East." Mona explained. "It's also in the court of the countries representing terrorist groups in the Middle East. And all of these nations are well aware of the danger that they could be bringing upon themselves should they not consider peace as a viable alternative. They are all well aware that this is, indeed, a high-stakes situation that the world has never seen before. I think that there are people of good conscience on all seven continents around the world who are keenly aware that we could be wrestling with Earth's final hope. So, we are taking measures to make sure that there are no escalations of violence, no provocations, or any interference that would hinder deals that need to be accomplished in the Middle East, in Europe, in Asia, in North and South America, or anywhere on Earth. The time for permanent international peace is now. We are hopeful that amiable diplomatic discussions will continue at all of the future negotiation tables. It is our hope that all nations will be willing to make whatever compromises and sacrifices are necessary to get the overall deal done. This is a matter that the entire world is watching. The alleviation of horrific, untold suffering and hardship on an extremely broad scale is at stake. President White, myself, Romeo Barone, and many members of our team have and will continue to meet with world leaders. Our intention is to detour them from their inclination of using Weapons of Mass Destruction as part of their strategy. The good news is that we are seeing more compliance abroad with National

Security Council resolutions. We are also observing less degrading of infrastructures of countries who are normally in opposition with one another, less desire to inflict losses and casualties, and a willingness to reduce terrorist attacks. Progress is being made by responsible parties. We are approaching a multilateral ceasefire and a broad diplomatic resolution. From the President on down, we will continue to stay in close touch will the families of the hostages who are now rescued and free. I've spent a lot of time with the families of the hostages who are now safe and also the families of hostages we intend to see released in the future. They have been both heartbreaking and uplifting conversations. And we are going to build on this foundation, deriving inspiration and courage to move forward with this imperative endeavor. We will maintain our momentum in getting the remainder of the hostages released, securing a worldwide ceasefire, and ultimately, ridding our planet of weapons that threaten our very existence. We earnestly appeal to all nations possessing nuclear and chemical weapons to uphold a standard of peace for everyone's sake, so that we may all wake up one morning to a good day of permanent international peace. We will diligently pursue the product of peace through ongoing, high-level, hard diplomacy to generate a great deal of humanitarian assistance to civilians around the world, the exit of thousands of endangered foreign nationals abroad including American citizens and restore all hostages safely to the loving arms of their families in many various countries. All of this has been the product of President White's leadership role in this massive endeavor of rescuing hostages and securing peace for our world. This is the course that President White has set us on and been vitally engaged in himself. The President could not be more clear about seeing this golden opportunity through. President White is going to continue to focus on what is going to produce results. All partners of the United States are working diligently to make peace a reality. And President White will be continuing to participate with us in future negotiation talks abroad. I will, of course, be conferring with the President very closely at the White House, Camp David, and upcoming summits. We will be monitoring the world climate closely during this entire process, always making quick determinations as to whether or not military action on the part of the United States is required. The upcoming summit meetings will be of the utmost international security focus on a global basis. There is strong bipartisan support from United States Congressional leaders to generate the freedom of all the remaining hostages, and funding is being proposed for a number of related priorities. All of our allies have pledged to sustain their commitment of contributing to this ongoing cause of lasting importance. We are all strong-willed in this tenacious effort to become single-minded in creating a less dangerous world. This is not the time to relax and rest on our laurels. While these developments are, indeed, favorable, we cannot be satisfied. We are constrained to approach this occasion as a door that may never open to us again. Once it closes, this door of opportunity may very well remain shut. It is not too dramatic to say that the entire world has never witnessed a realistic chance like this before in obtaining international peace. And we may never see it again. Therefore, there can be no room for miscalculation in our diplomatic approach in the immediate days to come. With an attitude of optimism, we will meet all obstacles to this noble goal in a pragmatic manner, establishing policies that will benefit all, without discrimination. There are many nations, once competitors of the United States, who are now choosing to annex with us in the cause of international peace. The NATO alliance is bigger, stronger, and more united than it has ever been. We have had and will continue to have good preparation as we press on to future summit meetings. And we look forward to seeing more and more allies join us in total unity, reflecting the type of burden sharing that has always been at the very heart of the NATO nation's collective vision. We have successfully secured the most complex hostage exchange in history. Hundreds of hostages from the four corners of Earth are finally coming home. This is a feat of diplomacy that could only be achieved by a leader like President Alexander Hampton White. At his direction, the professionals with our national security, foreign policy, and intelligence community worked tirelessly to secure the release of these individuals, many who have been in captivity for years and years. President White coordinated the final arrangements and caused everything to fall into place. We followed his lead, and we are all deeply grateful to our allies who supported the United States in these complex negotiations. And as I speak, President White is reaching out to extend his personal thanks to the many world leaders who have helped to make this momentous occasion possible. This was a concerted effort to rally allies to rescue and save lives from an unimaginable ordeal. And as this glorious result continues to unfold, we will never forget the remaining men, women, and children who need to be freed. We are diligently committed to see them all rescued. The release of the hostages who are free now has resulted in a very dramatic, positive shift in the right direction regarding the balance of power in our world. And as more hostages are released in days to come, this impetus will become stronger and more liberating. While hostile people are holding American hostages against their will, they are holding America hostage. Therefore, these legitimate rescue operations will continue with laser beam focus to free the remainder of our hostages. The hostages who have been rescued and restored to embrace their families and friends serve as fresh signals that permanent, international peace is on the horizon, with many nations considering a ceasefire proposal. This is a decisive moment for our entire world, putting everyone on a path of enduring, international peace. This is an intense diplomatic initiative of President White's leadership. It is time for this unprecedented opportunity to come to pass. We are making a concerted endeavor at every turn to prevent this glorious process from becoming derailed. All of these events have served to set the stage for what lies ahead. We are hopeful for a process that leads us all to an enduring peace, security, and stability. And when we have more to report with even greater definition, we will, of course, be sharing it with you. Thank you very much."

United States Secretary of State Mona Lisa Romano walked away from the State Department Daily Press Briefing Room podium with screaming correspondents desperately clamoring in an attempt to get more questions answered.

All during the diplomatic talks that Mona Lisa had been engaged in, she could not get the immortal words of her mentor, Dr. Abigail Grant, out of her mind: "There's pressure on both sides of the negotiating table, Mona." Mona thought to herself: "No truer words were ever spoken!"

Mona Lisa Romana, President Alexander Hampton White, Romeo Barone, Dr. Abigail Grant, and other people who were privy knew for a fact that the phenomenal events of the hostage negotiations and ceasefires were definitely being influenced by the Mona Lisa, Leonardo da Vinci's masterpiece. People were keenly aware the Mona Lisa was apparently working behind the scenes. It inspired them to know that a good force was reenforcing all their endeavors. And the negotiating team, including President White, all became accustomed to aligning themselves with this mystical power that was ensuring their success. Mona Lisa Romano would like to have been allowed the luxury of mentioning that the Mona Lisa was another major factor causing everything to fall into place. But this was a secret that Mona Lisa Romano would have to let the people of the world find out for themselves.

And everything naturally led up to what Mona Lisa referred to as a "courtesy call shuttle diplomacy summit" between the nations of Italy and France, that would take place in Paris. The relationship between Italy and France, in our modern age, was very friendly. It was only fitting that cooperation between these two major neighboring partners led them both to become founding members of the European Union. Mona Lisa Romano and Romeo Barone had good intentions of taking Italy and France's close economic, cultural, and historic ties even further, bolstering bilateral relations. Both Mona and Romeo sensed that it was perfect timing. They were in the right place at the right time.

As everyone associated with the friendly negotiations was about to have dinner one evening, Mona Lisa and Romano were seated at the head of the table across from each other, next to French President Regis Delon and Italian President Francesco Ferrari and their wives. There was a French waiter and waitress standing at the other end of Mona and Romeo's table, and they simultaneously could not help but notice the way that Mona and Romeo were looking at each other.

"Ah, amore! Amore! I know that's an Italian word, but under the circumstances, it's most proper. Amore!" The French waiter said to the French waitress.

"It's quite obvious, Fabien. That's Amore, all right!" The French waitress very happily confirmed.

The exquisite dinner was served, and there was an atmosphere of complete frivolity and revelry in the banquet room.

"I am the man who accompanied Mona Lisa Romano to Paris, and I've enjoyed it. I couldn't resist saying that," Romeo announced, as everyone within the sound of his voice broke out in a crescendo of laughter.

"Ah, yes. President John F. Kennedy referring to his wife Jacqueline Bouvier Kennedy on their visit to Paris." French President Delon could not help but recall.

"They made a tremendous impression upon the people of France!"

"President Delon, the Pope has been most gracious to invite Mona to speak at St. Peter's Basilica at the Vatican in Rome as part of this diplomatic trip. I wonder if you may be open to the idea of loaning the Mona Lisa portrait that's currently at the Louvre Museum here in Paris to be exhibited at St. Peter's Cathedral as Mona speaks. It would be a tremendous gesture of goodwill toward the Italian people, as Leonardo da Vinci, who painted the Mona Lisa, did come from Italy. In fact, Leonardo worked at the Vatican for a while. Surely, your kind gesture of allowing the Mona Lisa to be exhibited in the White House was greatly appreciated by President White, his wife, and the American people. All the more, it would be a kindness enjoyed by President Ferrari, his wife, and the Italian people," Romeo enquired, exercising some fast-on-his-feet-diplomacy, practically holding his breath after he asked. It showed to some at the banquet table that Romeo was making his heartfelt request for Mona Romano's welfare as well. Romeo Barone, by this time, had already had many conversations with Dr. Abigail Grant and President White concerning Mona.

French President Delon and Italian President Ferrari looked at each other at the same time. Suddenly, glowing smiles appeared on both of their faces.

"But of course!" President Delon responded whole-heartedly, with everyone surrounding him nodding in approval.

"I think that's a wonderful idea. What better way could there be to further improve relations even more between France and Italy?"

Leonardo Da Vinci International Airport

Air Force One could not have possibly looked any more majestic as the plane taxied down the runway toward the airport. Throngs of Italian citizens who had heard of the success of the diplomatic visit in France, packed the airport in hopes of getting a glimpse of Mona Lisa and Romeo upon their arrival to Rome, Italy.

Air Force One Taxiing Runway In Rome, Italy

Romeo was doodling with a musical listening device on the plane that had the capability of playing any song that had ever been produced. Out of all the poetic ballads Romeo could have chosen, rather than picking a melody in a serendipitous manner, he decided on a very specific, favorite tune, "When It's Love," by Van Halen, with the lyrics:

"How do I know when it's love? I can't tell you, but it lasts forever. How does it feel when it's love? It's just something you feel together. Oh, when it's love."

Mona Lisa took Romeo by the hand.

"I'm not sure it's appropriate to have a rock concert on board Air Force One, Romeo," Mona Lisa said sweetly, with her alluring smile.

"Hey! When in Rome, Mona!" Romeo happily responded.

Mona Lisa could not help but laugh.

"Romeo, Romeo. Where for art thou, Romeo?" Mona Lisa mused.

The Vatican — St. Peter's Cathedral (Basilica) In Rome With The Mona Lisa Portrait Exhibited — Televised Worldwide

The Vatican — St. Peter's Square — Rome, Italy

"Mona Lisa Romano belongs to Italy." The Pope began as he introduced Mona to thousands and thousands of people who gathered that evening at the Basilica. The Pope had just given Mona a key to the city, officially acknowledging her as a citizen of Rome.

"We are all very pleased with the magnificent strides of diplomacy that Mona Lisa has procured in our world. Mona Lisa is a warrior and champion for peace. Her courage has made it possible for many people in our world to not have to live in fear of war, dissension, and poverty. Mona Romano and her entourage are to be commended for their daring hostage negotiation successes. The wonderful seed that Mona has sown will surely reap a great harvest. It is the desire of all good people in our world to bring unity to the Earth. Therefore, it is with great joy, love, and anticipation that I present to you the First Lady of Rome, as her last name literally means 'citizen of Rome,' United States Secretary of State Mona Lisa Romano."

The crowd met Mona Lisa's approach to the podium with a roar of applause. It reverberated an incredibly intense vibration. St. Peter's Square was jammed like never before. United States Deputy Secretary Romeo Barone was seated on the platform. The Mona Lisa portrait was prominently displayed directly behind the podium where Mona Lisa Romano was about to speak.

"Thank you!" Mona said in all sincerity to the Pope and the enthusiastic crowd.

"I've always felt that I am a citizen of Rome, Italy, and I couldn't feel any more tightly knit to such a wonderful company of people. I have derived a great deal of joy from visiting the city of Rome. And the greatest honor of my life is to officially be recognized as one of your citizens at St. Peter's Cathedral here at the Vatican. I will forever cherish this key to the city of Rome that you have given to me. I am greatly honored by your kindness.

THE MONA LISA PORTRAIT DISPLAYED

AT THE VATICAN IN ROME, ITALY

As we come together in a spirit of comradery, it is very safe to say that we are all united as citizens of Rome! And I need to add that United States President, Alexander White, Italian President, Francesco Ferrari, and French President, Regis Delon all extend their warmest regards to everyone. And we can all extend our personal thanks to French President Delon for the inspiration of the Mona Lisa portrait being present with us today in her home country of Italy."

The swarm of people, representing folks from all nationalities, spontaneously burst out with cheers, tears of joy, and applause.

"Today, we stand at a crossroads where all the nations of Earth are indispensable components of the international system, no longer tempered by a daunting, hard, and bitter peace. Our motivation and impetus for the association of all countries is the mutual benefit of permanent, all-encompassing world peace and concrete values of integrity, such as honesty, reliability, and transparency. We, as a people, will no longer tolerate the dangerous existence of so many diametrically opposed world orders living under the umbrella of separate international orders. We, as a people, will no longer accept the dichotomy of friendly coexistence prevailing between many nations of our world while looming, adverse confrontation overshadows the remainder of the landscape. We desire a lasting, multilateral, win-win scenario for all the nations of Earth. We acknowledge that the days of mudslinging among nations are over so that we may devote our efforts to the challenge of creating a genuinely balanced equilibrium and unity that will serve to successfully override the dark side of our current human condition that's attempting to prevent us from avoiding an ultimate nuclear weapons showdown. Our pure motive collectively is to manifest what is good, just, and right for all concerned. Our imperative priority is to establish an unshakable trust among all the nations of the world. All of our struggles, all of our misunderstandings, all of our conflicts, all of our setbacks, all of our disappointments, and all of the pain that has ever been inflicted upon the human race have led us to the pinnacle of realizing that we are engaged in an international dilemma that must be resolved. Otherwise, the very process that has brought us to this place will inevitably serve to destroy ourselves. We rather are seeking acceptance, validation, and friendship among each other. We, as human beings, desire to exclusively reflect and project the positive attributes of being human beings and move forward, leaving behind every last bit of the negativity that has brought history to this point. As United States President John F. Kennedy put it in his commencement address at American University in Washington, D.C., in June of 1962: 'No government or social system is so evil that its people must be considered as lacking in virtue.' And directly as a result of examining our attitude toward freedom around the entire world, our reward for the acquisition of permanent, ongoing international peace will bequeath the virtues that shall be instilled within us all through the progressive, interdependent steps of our unrelenting endeavors. It was also John F. Kennedy who said: 'We are not here to curse the darkness. We are here to light a candle.' The alleged weak things of this world, hence, our devotion to unity among each other, will confound the things that were once considered mighty, that is, the prior rivalries and hatred that the hopeless side of our human nature has put on public display in our history books. Our own personal introspection will cause us all to recognize our desperate need for change, causing us to throw off our former selves for the sake of advancement for the entire human race. Our intentions are not self-centered national interests but universal unity. We desire to be a peaceful people worldwide who love liberty and the rights of men, women, and children more than we love anything else. And based on this very premise, we are a people in agreement for the common good and productive welfare of each and every nation in our world. We feel this admirable goal is the crowning achievement of human civilization and our last, best hope for Earth."

The Vatican — St. Peter's Square — Rome, Italy

"Mona Lisa! Mona Lisa! Mona Lisa!" The crowd kept shouting out, with lit candles in their hands.

"We seek the power that will enable us all to become greater in scope and purpose than any previous human endeavor for progress. Many previous attempts to establish peace in the past through high-stakes negotiations, foreign policy, and diplomacy have miserably failed because we have been incapable of overruling our own shortcomings and, as a direct result, defeated our own purpose. Our course here today will shape the destiny of mankind. We possess the keen awareness that creating a strategic partnership that is successful will not just rely on proclamations of intent, but also need to be matched by specific steps in the agreed direction. In multilateral agreement and unanimity, this permanent balance of power will be a perfect balance for all nations. We all must realize that the international community shares the responsibility, with complete transparency, to ensure human rights for all through international action. No man is an island unto himself. Even in the cultural and social context, universal human rights do amount to a lot more than merely noble talk. In a manner that combines vision with courage, human rights indicate the significance that we are all born to be free and equal so that we may have the right to live with dignity. This standard of freedom will not be imposed upon anyone. We are determined to overcome the obstacles that prevent divergent cultures from becoming a harmonious entity. We know the devastating experiences that have hindered unity among the nations of Earth. Hindsight is 20/20, and we clearly understand the rhymes and the reasons of exactly why so much devastation has taken place in our world. That is not a mystery. What requires explanation is the appropriate direction we need to take to get ourselves out of this dilemma that we all face. And how is it possible to speed up this vast, dramatic transformation? Because right now it appears that all nations under heaven are in chaos! And we're living in a day when the cycle, which is endless, evolves from disequilibrium to equilibrium, and then, back to disequilibrium again. Many very sincere central governments have emerged throughout history under the banner of the Westphalian concept of world order with a global economic structure, attempting to fit into the international system, only to crash and burn in upheaval. The modern era requires our ingenuity to blend national interests amiably into the international organization. This will not come about as a result of one nation converting or forcing another nation to its way of thinking. Democracy must be realized on an individual basis, with all its benefits vividly comprehended. And collectively, our united discovery of genuine democracy will, indeed, free us all from oppression. Democracy in its purest form will have a profound effect in the future to inspire and uplift humanity. The indispensable power of democracy will serve to bring a partnership among the nations of Earth and make it possible to provide an effective framework for a peaceful interplay among the various national interests in our world. This will create an international system that will maintain and preserve a strong national and cultural identity. Every country will be regarded as a major country. There will be no subordinates. There will surely be a dazzling array of multilateral democracies in our midst, with an emphasis on equality rather than a hegemony based on dominance. The creation of a permanent, idealistic, peaceful international order in our world will transcend all the barriers that history has imposed to delay its arrival. And once this international peace has been established, any and all blockades to future improvements, breakthroughs, developments, advancements, and enhancements will cease, and you and I will have much more time to devote to our creative abilities rather than having to develop more and more solutions for the problems presented by war, disease, and poverty. We will learn and appreciate one another's cultures. We will grow to understand the meaning of permanent, peaceful coexistence together. We will have mutual respect for each other's territorial integrity, and aggression among nations will be a thing of the past, never to be witnessed again. And because all countries will honor peaceful foreign policies, there will exist a friendly and cooperative position throughout the entire world. While every nation normally in the past has placed national interests first, world peace will now become the number one priority for the sake of mankind. The essence of this manifestation will, indeed, have a far-reaching influence. Metaphysical dynamics coupled with détente, the easing of hostility and strained relations between countries will bring about this global equilibrium. And our success will be measured by how much we maintain that standard of peace on Earth by not allowing ourselves to be drawn into conflict with each other. Our greatest joy will be finding out what is most advantageous for another country. Assisting our neighbors in reaching their goals will be made possible as we act on Westphalian Peace principle, practice democracy, and promote universal human rights. This is our opportune moment. Nuclear annihilation of the human race is the key issue. Self-destruction can be avoided. The inherent concern is self-preservation. We are a collection of nations potentially in permanent conflict with each other. But today, we have the option of world peace at our disposal before it's too late. The horrible consequences of war and the destruction of mankind have no reality. Reality lies in the peaceful coexistence of mankind. Therefore, we are not here today to raise monuments to our own importance but to acknowledge the fragility of our own human frailness. This pivotal moment in history will define permanent, international order as the acceptable definition of normality and be made possible by way of an active alliance policy. This imperative policy will be referred to as the Ultimatum Clause, serving as a final notice to the human race, challenging the nations of Earth and all their respective citizens to cease and desist once and for all from threats of any kind. Therefore, we are encouraged to adhere to proactive efforts of worldwide commitment conducive to a positive transformation in our world. We choose, with all our might, to exert an astonishing high-spirited energy of mutual assistance before a drastic, undesired balance of power inevitably takes us all to an inescapable point of no return. The Ultimatum Clause is an exert from the International Constitution of Democracy. This sacred constitution is fully expected to result in global peace for all nations, economic revival, and prosperity for the citizens of our world. The International Constitution of Democracy covets international stability among the governments on Earth and a guarantee of our survival from the weapons of mass destruction that mankind has produced. This is an event whose time has come, just as though our modern age contained a new, liberating narrative. The Westphalian sphere of influence, in its purest form, made up of equal members, is upon us in full force. Everything shall be based on the just laws of nature. There will be no distinction between the upper and lower classes, as the International Constitution of Democracy purports the inherent dignity of all humanity. The vision of unity will become a reality. The hope of freedom will come to fruition. The battle for peace has been won. And fulfillment of these goals has been secured on the basis of our involvement, not our withdrawal. It is vitally important that we're all engaged in the process of this unprecedented progression. No longer will negotiators on both sides of the table need to be concerned about different perspectives of world order and the substantial nuclear infrastructure that's been hanging over all of our heads like the sword of Damocles, threatening the existence of every last person in the civilized and uncivilized world. No longer will the international community need to fear an unfair balance of power in the world. No longer do we need to worry about a war being declared by various world orders. No longer will we need to be concerned about rulers who proclaim themselves to be the very embodiment of absolute power. No longer do we need to feel hopeless because world injustice has reached a point where peaceful methods are absolutely useless. No longer will we live in fear of an endless number of wars springing up all over Earth. No longer will we witness our helpless children become the innocent victims of war and senseless suffering. Now, we have a clear sense of direction. And we are compelled to head in that direction in a spirit of cooperation, placing a premium on endurance in sincerely desiring to establish relations of friendship with each other. The best for mankind is yet to come!"

The crowd went absolutely berserk. Everyone was still waving their lit candles in delirious joy. They kept chanting, "Mona Lisa! Mona Lisa! Mona Lisa!"

"We will be the fortunate ones who witness a massive change in our world in the future, and these developments will offer everyone a fresh outlook on life and a new global perspective, in vast comparison to the total disregard for human well-being and dignity has been the brutal, cruel mantra of certain totalitarian regimes. We have complete consciousness of the internal and external danger. The days of geopolitical, religious, and economic absolutism, allowing one ruler complete power and authority over a country or, potentially, the entire world, are over. Today, central to our fate and significant to our mutual benefit, we are billions of people held together in a beautiful mosaic pattern of harmonious rapport. It is with a clear understanding of each other's feelings and ideas that we search for and discover a permanent world order, absent of the consequences of political and religious conflict. Our main challenge is to keep peace in the equation as our center of gravity. We are fiercely loyal to this concept. We seek a guarantee of peace enduring enough for the nations of Earth to accept the existence of each other, allowing a worldwide ceasefire to be utterly declared, and for world leaders to seriously consider the dismantling of weapons of mass destruction to ensure the prospects of this ongoing peace that we insist upon. To reinforce the passion for the peace process, we desire concrete action that allows for diplomatic recognition of all countries. We seek to put a complete end to media, governmental, and educational campaigns that imply valid nations do not belong to the international community. We have traveled an anguished road on a journey toward an uncertain future. We have encountered those who are oblivious to human rights and seek only to misinterpret their sacred meaning. The purpose of humanitarian foreign policy is that we may all become allies. And in this New World of permanent world peace, we will be morally bound not to violate the universal principles of justice that keep us safe, just as much for our fellow neighbor as for ourselves. All utopian projects submitted in the past, claiming to subdue the opposing ideological clashes of history, have required extreme measures to implement. However, the dialogue of the

International Constitution of Democracy garners support for a smooth transition of world transformation to a universal system employing permanent, international peace and order. This peace will bring never-failing comfort to the citizens of Earth, causing urgency for all human beings on our planet to treat each other as human beings and to behave in a manner that brings dignity to other people as well as themselves. This transformation will, indeed, result in world unity and the improvement of everyone's welfare and well-being. The conundrum of international crisis brought about by threatening nationalist military autocracies will be a thing of the past. The wealth of energy and food resources will be combined to benefit every person in the world due to our overwhelming desire to treat our neighbors in a right and proper manner. Principal nuclear arms suppliers, even on the black market, and corrupt diplomatic advocates of ambitious, aggressive nationalist states will be shut down for good. All nations will be considered to be principal powers of influence as defenders and campaigners of peace. The process of laying this foundation will thwart all future wars and civil wars in every region of the world. Divergent political missions will dissolve as we focus on our collective assignment of upholding a sound international world order with the epoxy of peace. Universality has proven to be the most elusive to many conquerors in history. Perhaps they would have succeeded had they only included a permanent peace approach as the end result of their tactics and strategies. A peaceful world order depends on the ability to forge and expand unity among nations, overriding opposing points of view. And the one matter that we can all agree on is that we need peace in our world, peace that is here to stay. The most sincere, farsighted statemen have always known this fact, but, unfortunately, many of them did not live to see this reality come to pass. They were not allowed to witness the societies of the world transition from antagonistic villages to fruitful coexisting units thriving and interacting on peaceful terms. Diplomatic alignments have frequently been based on nations working together toward shared, significant goals. Our primary objective, for the sake of us all, is permanent peace on Earth. And justice shall prevail! No event in world history will equal the event of permanent world peace that our future has to hold. It will be this very adventure that will secure our ultimate victory in regard to freedom. At no time has the challenge of international peace been more complex than it is today. Now, the dream of the human race's future glory is coming into clear view, ensuring that the compatibility of all nations will align with the prospect of peace. This is the hope that will bring stability and limitless horizons to our entire world. We shall achieve unity, and each of us will define our global role as being peacemakers. Peace will be the source of the cooperative impetus that will guide and shape our strategic affairs globally, maneuvering us to a position of maximum advantage on the basis of international interest. Without peace, we cannot possibly endure the degree of diversity that is taking place in our world. In favor of a more direct approach, we shall witness a global sweep of international peace come to its ultimate fruition. All countries will be optimistic components of this world order. Accordingly, its statement will design international structures beneficial to all mankind, proposing international policies of democracy that are advantageous to one and all, maintaining the integrity of all nations and their citizens. The people of Earth will desire to do what is right for the common good of everyone. All policymaking will be performed on a platform of multilateral interest that is all inclusive. New ways of thinking about the nature of international order have culminated in our modern era. And today, we have chosen in earnest to weave the fabric of our international political structure by adjusting our differences through peaceful means. We publicly choose to denounce the annihilation of the human race. We need not be our own worst enemies. We believe this matter may be curtailed by our common shared values and productive development. We feel the grandest, most common-sense solution to a preemptive nuclear attack upon any nation is to not have nuclear, biological, or chemical weapons existing in any arsenal all around the world in the first place. As President Kennedy once emphatically stated in regard to international nuclear disarmament: 'The weapons of war must be abolished before they abolish us.' Peace is the factor that will proportionally shape the balance of power all around the globe."

Once again, those gathered at St. Peter's Basilica raged out of control, with the melodious mantra, holding lit candles: "Mona Lisa! Mona Lisa! Mona Lisa!"

"Permanent, international peace must be included in the equation of effective policy making. Peace is the essence of the international world order that is upon us. Peace is the key element of this emerging international structure that will never collapse. The task of a worthy statesman is to ensure that peaceful world order is established and sustain it once it has been achieved.

The psychological trauma that's associated with the nuclear arms race must come to a conclusive end. War has exhausted and drained the human race of all of our strength. By way of comparison, the international peace that is to come will be nothing but uplifting and strengthening to everyone. When we all agree to multilateral peace, all the other matters that concern us will fall into place. Everything will start to make sense. We will have a proper perspective like we never had before. We may even need to rewrite many of the books in our libraries. In the end, the businesses of military planning and diplomacy will not be remembered. But the beginning of permanent international world peace will not ever be forgotten for the subsequent generations to come.

Nevertheless, diplomacy, at this very moment, has become a matter of life and death. Only diplomacy that results in permanent world peace counts. This resulting peace will teach us how to hold together all the many races, peoples, and languages of Earth in a unified, cohesive structure, causing us to become respectful of the diversity of the many heritages, faiths, and customs that are represented all around the world. The reality of the Universal Code of Peace itself, along with its Universal Constitution of Democracy, will demonstrate to us that it is not an illusion. Peace alone will give us the solid principles and the sound reason to approach life with zeal for the best interests of mankind, embodying the spirit of this new age. It will be in this spirit that we will successfully avoid the war to end all wars, sometimes referred to as the apocalypse or Armageddon.

This is a timeless event, immersed in nature, that will dramatically change the world forever. Permanent, international peace will manage to cut through all the red tape to make global unity happen.

On November 22nd, 1963, President John F. Kennedy, had he been allowed to live, would have delivered a speech at the Trade Mart in Dallas, Texas. Toward the end of his speech, he concluded, 'We, in this country, in this generation, are by destiny rather than choice, the watchmen on the walls of world freedom. We ask, therefore, that we may be worthy of our power and responsibility, that we may exercise our strength with wisdom and restraint, and that we may achieve in our time and for all time the ancient vision of peace on Earth, goodwill toward all men. That must always be our goal.' As it is written: 'The lion shall lay down with the lamb. And they shall beat their swords into plowshares and their spears into pruning hooks. Nation shall not lift up sword against nation. Neither shall they learn war anymore.'"

Suddenly, from an eternally dynamic source, a tremendous power could be sensed from St. Peter's Cathedral, which reached out to the four corners of Earth. There came the sound of a rushing, mighty wind. And it managed to impact and permeate every molecule in the world with a positive endowment that affected every single person on the face of the planet.

Eventually, everyone in the world came to realize the secret that the Mona Lisa, created by Leonardo da Vinci, knew all along. She was well aware that there would one day be international peace on Earth. The love created was derived from the joy of all nations coming into perfect alignment with each other.

All the world leaders had such a change of heart that they ordered their militaries to completely dismantle and destroy weapons of any kind that could bring harm to human beings. United States President Alexander Hampton White delegated the same orders to his Joint Chiefs and Staff and all those involved, putting all of these military leaders out of a job. People no longer had a desire to kill. In fact, everyone completely lost their propensity to hurt another person or animal. All the criminals in the world threw down their weapons. Policemen turned in their guns to be destroyed. Weapons of any kind on Earth were done away with. Wildlife hunters no longer had a desire to kill innocent animals of nature. Even kids were throwing their slingshots and BB guns in the trash. The entire world would never be the same again. The true harmony of human beings was becoming realized. Everyone on the planet, very simply put, just had a sincere inclination to get along with each other. The hearts of everyone in the world have changed for the better. People, without hesitation or reservation, actually demonstrated a genuine, ongoing concern for the welfare of all other human beings, now having the capacity and propensity to do so. And with united hearts, a strong, healthy, healing rapport developed an eternal bond among every citizen of the universe. Genuine interconnections were established among all the nations of Earth. And love triumphed as the official music of the entire universe. Nature had made an ultimate, lasting connection with humanity. War no longer was the accepted norm. Peace was now the new standard that everyone happily lived by. Peace was having its way throughout all aspects and every scenario of life. No one knew the meaning of the word 'animosity.' And this international peace became more and more coveted by the world's society with the passage of time.

What the human race did not want for itself was thrust upon every man, woman, and child. People didn't want peace, but they got it anyway. And just like that, there was permanent world peace, courtesy of the Mona Lisa, who was created by the genius, Leonardo da Vinci. The nations of Earth had awakened to a brand-new world.

\

11

The White House, Washington, D.C.

"Mr. President, there's something unprecedented taking place all around the world. Scientists all over Earth are receiving an influx of information that's providing them with conclusive, provable answers about every mysterious anomaly that has ever baffled people. I, personally, can even tell you what happened to Amelia Earhart," Senior Presidential Aide Phoenix Anderson declared, as he stormed into the Oval Office of the White House.

234

President White, With His Senior Presidential Aide

"Where is the information coming from?" The President asked.

"No one, at this point, can explain the source of the information, Mr. President. But I have a file folder on it to give you a synopsis of what's happening," Phoenix said in an alarming tone of voice.

The Senior Presidential Aide handed the file folder to President White across his desk. President White opened the file folder, and read its contents with an expression on his face like he was trying to make sense of it all. After scanning the details as carefully as he could, he looked back to Pheonix Anderson with an expression of utter shock.

"The scientists know what happened to all the lost civilizations that disappeared in history without explanation, like the Sumerians in Mesopotamia, the Anasazi of the American southwest, the Indus Valley civilization in Pakistan in northwest India, just to name a few, along with insight of what became of the declining populations of Easter Island, the ancient Maya Empire in Mexico and Central America, the Khmer Empire of Cambodia, Laos, Thailand, and Vietnam, and all the rest. Now, we know who created Gobekli Tepe in Turkey and the 700 geoglyphs in the Nazca Desert in Southern Peru. The scientists have a clear understanding and interpretation of the WOW Signal. They know all about the signals being sent from the M-83 Galaxy. They can tell us everything about the pyramids of Giza and the Great Sphinx of Giza. The Mexican pyramids in Teotihuacan are no longer a mystery, as well as all the other pyramids in the world, including the Antarctica pyramids. They know where the Ark of the Covenant and the Holy Grail are located. We know everything about the Loch Ness Monster now. The Bermuda Triangle and Stonehenge in England have totally been explained. They can tell us everything about the Moth

Man sightings in West Virginia. And scientists around the world have a thorough understanding of the Great Attractor, the region of gravitational attraction in intergalactic space and the apparent central point of the Laniakea Supercluster, which is home to the Milky Way and approximately 100,000 other nearby galaxies. The Great Attractor's massive gravitational force is pulling the Earth towards it, along with the entire Milky Way, to where our local galactic neighbor resides. All the questions we've had about the Moon have been completely answered. The scientists have a thorough understanding of all this and much, much more. Oncologists are receiving effective treatment information to cure all the hundreds of different types of cancer, Mr. President. Primary Care Physicians and all medical Specialists are being relayed healing remedies for every kind of chronic disease known to man, along with preventive medicine measures to prevent these diseases from ever occurring. There will never be another pandemic again caused by a virus. We now even know how to alleviate the common cold. This is unbelievable! This list goes on and on and on. It's endless!" The President exclaimed.

"It is endless, Mr. President! The information that's pouring in is absolutely endless!" Phoenix exclaimed. "And what you have in your hands is just a small tip of the iceberg! Also, President White, of course, since all nuclear weapons have been dismantled and destroyed, there's no method remaining to obliterate incoming asteroids. But scientists, through this influx of information, have developed a more foolproof method of blasting asteroids that threaten the Earth. Nuking the asteroids was limited anyway. But at the same time, the scientists are stating that this new organization that's taking place in the universe is reconfiguring everything so beautifully that we may never have the threat of an asteroid hitting the Earth again," Phoenix stressed.

"Well, it certainly, appears that that everything is falling into its proper place, all right. Perhaps we can persuade Congress to pass an Amendment so a United States President can preside in office for as many consecutive terms as the American people see fit," President Alexander Hampton White concluded in jest.

12

Mona Lisa Romano And Romeo Barone

After their eventful visit to Italy, Romeo Barone and Mona Lisa Ramona mutually decided to get away from it all so they could pause and reflect. Mona Lisa was regarded by everyone on Earth to be a venerable stateswoman. Just like her parents had predicted when they named her at birth, Mona Lisa Romano had become even more famous than the Mona Lisa portrait. Romeo and Mona Lisa were firmly embracing each other under an extraordinarily large, full Moon as the waves of the Atlantic Ocean came crashing to the shore of Manhattan's Atlantic Beach, very close to where the two companions were standing. They were so consumed with passion that they were both oblivious to any risk of the high waves that were pounding the beach. Mona and Romeo were reveling in each other.

"Well, Mona Lisa, there may be a Nobel Peace Prize in this for you." Romeo sweetly pointed out to his girlfriend.

"I suppose it's true that the pen is mightier than the sword, my dear Romeo." Mona retorted as she playfully tilted her head and body backward, then returned forward as she depended upon the leverage of Romeo's embrace. As Mona came in close to Romeo, he took the opportunity to kiss her.

"That was a good kiss!" Romeo couldn't help but notice.

"I don't see anything wrong with any of them." Mona whimsically responded, yet meaning it with all of her heart.

"It just seems perfectly natural being with you like this," Romeo remarked.

"It's definitely apropos." Mona tenderly responded.

"We can't be too careful. There's a full Moon out this evening, Mona Lisa." Romeo heeded.

"Yeah, but it's a romantic full Moon tonight!" Mona Lisa joyfully discerned with a mischievous, enigmatic smile, safe in the close, intimate, caring cuddle and caress of Romeo's arms.

Made in the USA
Columbia, SC
12 June 2025